TAKING A CHANCE

OAK BROOK ACADEMY, BOOK 6

JILLIAN ADAMS

JILLIANADAMS.COM

ONE

I closed my computer and sighed as I sat back in my chair. The library was empty. Not surprising, since it was going to close in a few minutes and most of the other students at Oak Brook Academy had other plans for a Friday night.

I'd turned down a few invitations to spend time at the library, using the excuse that I had a test to study for. I did have a test, but I didn't need to study for it. It was in my easiest class and I had no doubt that I'd pass. I just didn't want to wander around being the only person in my group of friends who didn't have a hand to hold.

At times it didn't bother me, but lately, it had been grating on my nerves. It didn't help that the people who swore they would never fall in love in high school had actually fallen in love. Not in easy love either, but in the kind of love that books were written about.

Me, on the other hand? I'd just been reading the books. I was the one who lay awake at night imagining what it would be like to get swept off my feet.

I didn't have very high standards for love. He didn't need to be handsome or rich or even terribly modern. I just longed for that flutter in my chest and that look in his eyes.

I'd tried and failed a few dozen times. I'd take any attention I could get and hope that it would lead to something close to romance. But it usually didn't.

He would try to kiss me and my forehead would knock into his. He would try to hold my hand right after I'd blown my nose. He would take me to a movie full of gore that I couldn't even sit through. He would ask me to do his homework.

None of my relationships worked out and none were even close to being romantic. But unlike my friends—many of whom had rejected the idea of love altogether after facing some difficulties—I still wanted to jump in with both feet.

Annoyed by my wandering down Loves Lost Lane, I decided I'd had enough of the library. I snapped my book closed and stood up from the table. Maybe my romance would only ever just be fantasy, but at least I had the fantasies to hold onto. Hopefully they would at least get me to college.

As I stepped out of the library, a cool breeze rustled through my hair. The quiet of the courtyard seemed welcoming to me. I'd heard all the lectures from my grandmother about not being out alone at night, but Oak Brook gave me a sense of safety that kept my nerves from being on edge. Here, I was home and no one had any interest in hurting me.

No one had any other interest in me either, but that was something I just had to deal with.

I wasn't like the other students that attended the upscale boarding school. Although my grandmother had plenty of money due to her fashion empire, she never let that go to my head.

The home she'd raised me in after my parents passed away was modest. Our life had never extravagant. She taught me that with great wealth came great responsibility, and although I might have the perks of life—such as a fantastic education—I always needed to be aware of what others didn't have so that I might be able to change things in the future.

I did want to change things. But not necessarily for people. I had a strong passion for the protection of nature and animals.

One of the few trips that my grandmother had taken me on had been to the rain forest. I'd learned so much over that two-week vacation that I'd come home energized with the desire to find a way to protect it and other natural wonders around the world. Since then, I'd been driven to raise money and gather support for the protection of animals and natural spaces.

Unfortunately, the average Oak Brook Academy student couldn't be bothered with concern for the environment.

As I strolled through the courtyard, I listened for the familiar sound of crickets, one of the few elements of nature that could survive in the big city. I didn't hear them, however, because another sound drowned them out. A sharp grating sound that set my nerves on edge.

"Hello?" I peered around the courtyard in search of the source of the sound. Was it some kind of power tool? A drill? It seemed odd for anyone to be doing maintenance in the dark.

The sound stopped and an unfamiliar voice greeted me from behind one of the statues: "Who's there?"

"Uh—I asked first?" I shoved my hands in my pockets and shivered as another breeze ruffled through my hair. "What are you doing?" I could tell from the sound of the voice that he was about my age, but the statue blocked any other details I might be able to discern about the person.

"You never saw anything!" the voice called out, then I heard footsteps as he started to run off.

"Okay?" I frowned as I walked around the side of the statue. I pointed the flashlight on my camera at the statue and gasped. What once was a serene face had been drilled into something much more sinister. "Why would you do this?" I turned and looked in the direction that I'd seen the boy run off in.

I caught sight of a flash of light rounding the building that housed the dormitories.

Determined to find out who was responsible for such a terrible thing, I chased after the flicker of light. The faster I ran, the happier I was that I'd joined the track team earlier in the year. The practice helped me catch up to the boy fairly quickly.

"Seriously? You're chasing me?" He glanced back over his shoulder but bolted forward a second later.

He moved too fast for me to get a good look at his face.

I continued to run after him.

"You shouldn't have done that! It's school property!"

He stopped at the edge of the campus beside a known gap in the fence where some of the less than honest kids snuck off into the city when they felt like it.

"Oh, so sorry about that, I guess I'm going to have to feel guilty about it for the rest of my life." He laughed, then ran through the opening.

I ran up to it but stopped short of going through it. I wasn't much of a rule breaker. I didn't want to end up getting into trouble just to chase down someone whom I most likely couldn't catch anyway.

Annoyed, I considered calling security. But what would I tell them? I had no idea who the person was or even what he looked like.

Instead, I walked back to the statue.

As I looked over the face again, I realized I didn't completely hate it. There was something a little satisfying about the distortion of the perfectly angelic expression that had once inhabited the statue's face.

I looked back over my shoulder again, but there was no sign of the boy returning. I snapped a picture of the statue, then continued toward my dorm. At least my night had been a little more eventful than I'd first expected.

I was almost at the door when I felt a hand grab my arm.

"Watch it!" I jumped back and raised a fist in the direction of the person who'd touched me.

"Easy now." Apple grinned. "You're not going to knock me out, are you?"

"No." I offered a nervous laugh. "Sorry, I'm a little spooked tonight."

"Let's get inside then." Apple walked with me through the door of the dormitories.

Once inside, I stopped just for a second and looked back out through the window.

Soon enough everyone at the school would know about the destruction of the statue. Would the culprit come forward then?

TWO

I closed my eyes. Maybe if I stopped staring at the ceiling, I'd be able to go to sleep. Ever since I'd arrived in my dorm room, I'd tried to stop thinking about what had happened in the courtyard. But my thoughts bounced right back to that stupid laugh. He was so smug because he knew he was going to get away with it.

And I'd let him, hadn't I? I'd just let him run off.

Annoyed, I turned over in my bed and punched my pillow. Maybe if I'd followed him, I'd be able to sleep. That's how it had always been with me.

When it came to confrontation, I'd run the other way. Why not? Most situations weren't worth the stress.

But this one? I loved the statues in the courtyard. Each one represented a value held dear by the founders of Oak Brook Academy. Why would anyone want to destroy something like that?

Finally, I gave up on trying to sleep. I climbed out of bed and walked over to my window. It overlooked the courtyard. Everything was dark, making it impossible to find the statue that had been damaged.

As I continued to search, I noticed a flicker of a flashlight beam.

My heart skipped a beat. It had to be him. No one else would be out in the courtyard at this hour. I bit into my bottom lip and wondered if I should stay in my safe and warm dorm room. It would be the easier thing to do. But I had a chance to catch the person who'd damaged the statue—to eliminate his smug attitude.

I bolted out of my room and then out into the hallway. I raced down the stairs and through the common room out into the courtyard.

It didn't occur to me that I was in my pajamas until my bare feet hit the cold cobblestone that lined the courtyard. I hesitated for a moment as I considered going back for shoes and some decent clothes, but I knew that I might miss my chance to catch him.

I swept my gaze across the courtyard in search of the flashlight beam.

Finally, I spotted it flickering along the wall of the boys' dormitory.

I broke into a run in an attempt to catch him before he could go in the side entrance. I caught sight of a shadowy figure making his way around the side of the building. "Wait! Come back here!"

He spun around to face me and shined his flashlight directly into my eyes.

"Ouch! Stop!" I held my hand in front of my face to block the beam.

"Me stop?" He chuckled. "You're the one stalking me. Should I be afraid?" He ran the beam of the flashlight along the silky material of my pajamas, which were dotted with sleepy sheep. "What's wrong, Little Bo Beep, did you lose one of your sheep?"

"Is that supposed to be funny?" I glared at him. His face was still half-hidden in the shadows, but I caught a glimpse of the curve of his lips.

"I'm certainly laughing." He smirked as he crossed his arms. "What are you doing out this late, Princess?"

"I was looking for you." I scowled at him. "I saw what you did earlier."

"What I did?" He tipped his head to the side and looked into my eyes. "I don't know what you think you saw, but maybe you should think again. The darkness can confuse a lot of people."

"I'm not confused." I took a step closer to him. "I know exactly what I saw."

"You should go back to bed." His voice hardened. "I'm sure lack of sleep is messing with your head."

"Not so smug now, are you? I saw which statue you damaged. I'm not going to shut up about it either." I held up my phone and snapped a picture of him before he could turn away. "Out past curfew and off campus without permission too. I'll bet all that is going to add up to a whole lot of problems for you."

"Delete that." He reached for my phone.

"Don't!" I yanked my hand back. "You're not so tough now, are you?"

"Do you want to see how tough I can be?" His hand landed on my shoulder.

I shivered and pulled back from his touch.

"Oh." He laughed again. "I see. You're not tough at all." He held his hand out toward me. "Give me your phone. I'll delete the picture and we can both forget any of this happened."

Frightened, I clutched my phone tightly and peered through the darkness at him. I still had no idea who he was. What if he was as dangerous as he pretended to be? Did I really want to get hurt or worse over a statue?

"Candace, right?" His tone remained stern.

A burst of cold rushed through me. He knew my name? Which meant he could hunt me down any time he wanted. Was that a risk I really wanted to take?

"Candace, give me the phone." He shifted closer to me, his fingertips extended to touch the back of my hand. "Don't make me take it from you." His voice softened just enough for me to notice.

"No." I drew my hand and my phone back. "Don't touch me."

"Relax." He slid his hands into his pockets. "We can work this out, can't we? You're right, you could cause me a lot of trouble with that picture. All you have to do is delete it and we can forget any of this ever happened. Alright?" He met my eyes.

"Alright." I shivered again as I pulled the picture up on my phone.

When I saw the face in the photograph, illuminated by the flash on my phone, my heart pounded. Nicholas Holden.

I'd never met him directly before, because we certainly didn't run in the same circles, but his reputation was a wicked one. No one knew how he hadn't been expelled from the school yet. Rumors spread through school that he was the child of royalty or someone extremely wealthy, because no matter what he did, he didn't get kicked out.

My finger hovered over the trash can icon on the bottom of the picture. Would it matter if I showed the principal the picture? He'd probably just get away with it again.

I glanced back up at him.

"Delete it." He looked straight into my eyes. "Then we can go back to pretending we never met."

I bit into my bottom lip. I wanted to be brave enough to shout at him. I wanted to insist that I'd get him kicked out of school once and for all. But I was no lion, I was just a mouse, like I'd always been.

"There." I cleared my throat as I held up my phone. "I deleted it."

"Let me see." He reached for my phone.

"Don't." I pulled my hand back again.

"Would you relax?" He rolled his eyes. "I can't believe you if I don't check for myself. What, do you have some kind of naked pictures on here or something?" He laughed as he snatched at the phone again.

"Of course not!" I glared at him, then reluctantly handed over the phone. I wanted more than anything for our encounter to be over.

"See? That wasn't so hard, was it?" He took the phone.

I watched as he tapped and swiped through it, then nodded and handed it back to me. "It looks like you were telling me the truth."

"I'm not the liar here." I tucked the phone into the pocket of my pajama pants.

"No, just the stalker." He tipped his head to the side. "Aren't good little princesses supposed to be in bed right now?"

"Aren't decent human beings not supposed to destroy other people's art?" I shuddered as I backed away from him.

"There's a big difference between art and brainwashing. You'll figure it out one day." He nodded toward the front of the building. "Go on. I'll make sure you get home safe."

I stared at him a moment longer, then started back around the side of the building.

I heard his footsteps a few feet behind me. I felt his eyes on me as I climbed the steps to the entrance of the dormitory. When I reached the door, I glanced back once and saw him not far from me.

He nodded again, then flicked his hand at me, encouraging me to go inside.

I shivered again. Was he really trying to be courteous by escorting me back to the dorms? Or was he just trying to intimidate me?

THREE

I woke up the next morning to the alarm on my phone buzzing directly beside my ear.

I winced and rubbed my eyes, then swatted at my phone until the alarm turned off.

"It's Saturday," I mumbled into my pillow. "No alarms on Saturday."

"Knock-knock!" Apple called out, knocking on the door. "This is your friendly wake-up reminder! It's the big day! Time to change the world!"

"Huh?" I rubbed my eyes again, then suddenly I remembered. Today the courtyard would be filled with tables and booths, each one supporting a different cause with the goal of retrieving huge donations from the wealthy students of Oak Brook.

I jumped out of bed and began to gather the literature I'd recently printed out. I pulled on my Save the Rain Forest t-shirt and gathered the free key chains I intended to hand out.

For the past two years I'd been involved in supporting the rain forest. The more I learned about it, the more involved I became. I preferred to spend most of my free time researching solutions to the problems. But today was my opportunity to rally others to the cause.

I smoothed my hair back into a ponytail, then grabbed a few of the signs I'd created. I headed for the door with boxes and signs in my arms.

"Breakfast!" Apple tossed a granola bar into one of the boxes. Then she opened the door for me.

"Thank you! Aren't you coming down?" I looked over her pajamas.

"You've already recruited me, remember? I'm going to support the cause of getting a little more sleep." She yawned, then headed back to her room.

I stumbled out through the door and managed to kick it closed behind me without dropping anything.

As I navigated the stairs, I expected to end up tumbling down them, but instead made it to the door that led to the courtyard. Only then did I pause long enough to remember what had happened the night before.

I looked through the door into the courtyard.

No, he wouldn't be up this early. We'd agreed to pretend that we'd never met. I hoped that he would stick to that agreement.

As I elbowed my way through the door, I tried to ignore the sensation of guilt that rippled through me. Why had I let him force me to delete the picture? I should have stood my ground and turned him in to the principal. Instead, I'd gotten scared and deleted the only evidence I had.

I dropped the boxes and signs in my spot in the courtyard. A few other people had begun to set up as well, but it was mostly still quiet.

"Morning, Candace!" A friend waved to me from across the courtyard.

"Morning, Holly." I smiled at her, then walked through the

courtyard. I wanted to take a serious look at the statue that had been damaged the night before.

As I walked around the statue, I noticed pieces of stone scattered across the cobblestone. The statue was of an angel with wings spread wide. The wings were apparently his target, as they had been drilled down to jagged nubs. He didn't touch the angelic face or the flowing robes, just the wings.

As I stared at what was left of the statue, my thoughts traveled back to what he'd said to me. Something about brainwashing. What could an angel statue have to do with brainwashing? Oak Brook Academy wasn't a religious school. Perhaps an angel wasn't the best choice for a statue, but it wasn't exactly offensive.

I snapped a picture, then tucked my phone back into my pocket.

"Do you know something about this?"

My heart skipped a beat as Ms. Lauren, my social studies teacher, stepped up behind me.

"No, nothing." I lowered my eyes.

"Nothing? Then why did you take a picture?" She frowned as she looked at me.

"I just thought it was odd." I shrugged.

"So you have no idea who did this?" She frowned. "This is a very valuable statue. The artist who created it is going to be devastated. I want to know everything I can about what happened here."

"No idea." I took a few steps back.

"Then why did I watch you walk right over to the statue? You didn't look at any of the other ones. No one else has come over to look at it. So why are you the only person that has an interest in this statue this morning?"

"I was just taking a walk around." I avoided her eyes. "I saw some of the crunched-up stone on the ground and I was curious where it came from. I'm sorry, Ms. Lauren, but I don't know any more than that."

"I'm sorry that I don't believe you." She glared at me as she crossed her arms. "I'm not going to let this go."

"I have to get back to my table." My heart pounded as I did my best to avoid looking directly at her. I didn't often lie to teachers. But what could I tell her? That I knew exactly who did it? I didn't want to have a boy like Nicholas as my enemy.

"Go on." Ms. Lauren pursed her lips. "But don't think that this conversation is over. It's not even close to being over."

I hurried back to my spot in the courtyard.

As I set up my table, I tried not to think about Ms. Lauren's warning. Would she be able to find out that I really did know something? That, in fact, I knew exactly who'd done it?

With my stomach in knots, I finished setting up. The courtyard had begun to fill up with colorful booths and tables. I distracted myself by decorating my table with pictures of the rain forest and the endangered animals within it.

Once finished, I settled behind the folding table and looked across the courtyard at the other tables that had been set up. Most of them had a long line of students ready to get more information and free accessories, and to sign petitions.

My table, on the other hand, had not one single soul in line for it.

"I guess not too many people are interested in saving the rain forest this year." I sighed and sank down further in my chair. It wouldn't be long until my friends arrived, signed my petition, then moved on. I wasn't sure that they supported the cause, but they always went out of their way to support me.

Maybe the problem was that my heart wasn't in it today. My thoughts were filled with the statue, Ms. Lauren, and unfortunately, Nicholas Holden. Even just the memory of him with his hand on my shoulder was enough to make my skin crawl.

I closed my eyes and decided to replace my terrible thoughts with some more pleasant ones.

What if a handsome stranger just happened to walk up to my table? What if he took one look in my eyes and asked me where I'd been all his life?

I melted at the thought. Yes, that would certainly distract me from any troubling thoughts. Would he be tall? Would he be funny?

I let my imagination wander until I heard footsteps close to my table. My eyes fluttered open just as a cloud drifted away from the sun. The sudden brightness caused me to reach up to shield my eyes.

The figure in front of my table leaned forward enough for me to recognize him.

"Hey there, Princess."

His voice grated at my nerves. The nickname inspired a sharp rage within me. *Not now. If I just don't look at him, he might go away.*

But it was already too late for that. His eyes had locked to mine.

FOUR

"I have nothing to say to you." I lowered my hand and leaned back in my chair.

"I'm just here for a key chain." He fished through the bowl on my table and plucked out one of the key chains.

I reached up and snatched it out of his grasp.

"Those are for people who sign the petition."

"Oh?" He raised an eyebrow as he smiled.

Why did he have to be handsome? It seemed to me that the troublemakers always were.

"Yes. They're not just free for the taking." I pulled the bowl back toward me.

"But the sign says free." He pointed to the small sign I'd attached to the bowl.

"Never mind, just please go away. Other people may want to sign the petition and donate." I shifted the empty donation jar closer to the front of the table.

"How much do I have to donate for the key chain?" He pulled a thick wallet from his back pocket.

"Just stop." I rolled my eyes. "What do you even want?"

"I saw you talking to Ms. Lauren." He flipped his wallet

open and pulled out a twenty-dollar bill. He tossed it into the jar.

I narrowed my eyes. I wanted to tell him to take it back, but it wasn't for me, was it?

"I didn't tell her anything if that's what you're worried about."

"I wasn't worried." He tossed another twenty into the jar. "Is that enough for a key chain?"

"Here, just take what you want." I thrust the bowl at him. "Just please, go away."

"Ouch." He chuckled as he tossed another twenty into the jar. "I'm getting a very harsh message from you. It's almost like you don't like me or something." He shrugged.

I stared down at the brochures strewn across my table and took a calming breath. I couldn't let him get under my skin. I needed to focus on the task at hand. I needed to bring awareness to the plight of the rain forest, not get distracted by an irritating person like him.

"Thank you very much for your donation." I picked up one of the pamphlets. "Please read this and direct any future donations to the account listed in the brochure."

"I'm not interested in a brochure." He tossed it back down on the table. "But if you'd like to tell me about it, I'll listen."

"No thank you." I cleared my throat as I looked past him. Maybe if someone would just walk up to the table, he would leave me alone. There were a lot more students in the courtyard, but none that seemed interested in my table.

"Save the rain forest!" I waved my hand through the air. "Please stop by my table and have a look at the latest numbers! We all have to pitch in to help!"

"I'm right here." He rested his hands on the table and looked at me. "Don't you want my signature?"

"I don't think a criminal has much interest in saving the rain forest."

"Then you think wrong." He plucked the pen from the clipboard, then jotted his name across the first empty line. "Maybe you should open your eyes and your heart a little bit. You might see more than just what everyone tells you to see."

"More than someone who destroyed a piece of art with a cordless hand drill?" I met his eyes. "Did you steal that?"

"If that's all you see, then you're just as blind as the rest." He tossed the pen back down on the clipboard. Then he added another twenty to the pile in the jar on my table. "You're welcome, by the way."

"The rain forest thanks you." I forced a smile.

"But not you, huh?" He raised an eyebrow. "I guess I'll just have to accept that you would prefer to keep your eyes closed."

"Maybe you should put up your own table." I shrugged. "If your message is so important to you, you could spread it to the rest of the students. I'm sure someone would be willing to listen."

"I'm not interested in spreading it to anyone else." He shook his head. "I don't give up easily."

"You should, because you're wasting your time." I glared at him. "What do you want with me anyway? I told you, I didn't tell anyone about what you did."

"And what exactly did he do?" Ms. Lauren stepped up to my table with a tight smile on her lips. "Please, fill me in, Candace."

I sank down in my chair and held my breath. I could feel his eyes on me. I could feel her eyes on me too. What was I supposed to do? Continue to lie?

My chest tightened at the thought. All I'd wanted to do was support a good cause, and instead, I was caught in an impossible situation.

"Candace?" Ms. Lauren looked between Nicholas and me. "Aren't you going to speak up?"

"I don't have anything to say." I looked down at the brochures on the table. "Would you like to make a donation to protect the rain forest and the endangered animals within it?" I offered one of the brochures to her.

"No, thank you." She ignored the brochure. "I'd like to know what exactly Mr. Holden did that you don't want to tell me about. You have ten seconds to start talking. After that you will officially have weekend detention."

"Weekend detention?" I gasped as I stared into her eyes. "Is that even a thing?"

"It is, if neither of you speaks up." She turned her attention to Nicholas. "Maybe you'd like to confess?"

Nicholas's jaw tensed as he stared hard at the ground. His lips didn't move.

"Okay, the countdown starts now." Ms. Lauren counted each second with a sharp tap of her fingertip against the table.

My heart pounded even faster with each tap of her finger. I felt the words rise to the tip of my tongue. All I had to tell her was what she obviously already suspected. So why couldn't I bring myself to do it?

I forced myself to look at Nicholas. He hadn't moved a muscle. His cheeks appeared flushed and his eyes narrowed, but he didn't speak or make a sound.

"Two, one." Ms. Lauren struck the table with a closed fist and sighed. "That's it. Close up shop, young lady, and report to the library." She looked straight at Nicholas. "You too."

"Wait, Ms. Lauren." Nicholas turned to face her. "This is unreasonable. You have no evidence to accuse either of us of any wrongdoing."

"You're right, I don't." She crossed her arms. "Luckily for me, this is a private school that doesn't require proof of guilt to enforce punishment. I am quite aware that the two of you know something about what happened to that statue last night. I'm not about to let you get away with it. That was an expensive piece of art and a valued part of Oak Brook Academy's culture." She looked between us once more, then leaned closer to me. "Last chance, Candace."

I chewed on my bottom lip as sweat dripped down my forehead. I hated being in trouble. But the thought of exposing Nicholas, with him standing right there in front of me, scared me more than weekend detention.

"I have nothing to say." My voice trembled as I spoke.

"Wonderful." Ms. Lauren shook her head. "Be in the library in ten minutes or you will face harsher consequences. Both of you." Ms. Lauren shot a glare in Nicholas's direction.

I fought back tears as I began to pile up the brochures on the table.

"Here, I'll help you." Nicholas grabbed some of the brochures and his hand brushed against mine as he did. I jerked my hand back as a strange burst of electricity carried through it.

"Don't bother. I can do it myself."

FIVE

"I've got this." He grabbed one end of the table.

"Don't." I glared at him.

"Look, what did you want me to do? Confess?" He sighed as he flipped the table over to fold it up. "I've got enough on my record to get myself kicked out of here."

"And whose fault is that?"

"You don't know anything about me." He shook his head. "It's easy to make assumptions, isn't it?"

"I'm not making any assumptions. Everything I need to know about you, I learned last night." I picked up my boxes and signs. "I'd prefer it if we just didn't speak to each other. Would that be so bad?"

"I guess not." He frowned as he propped the table against the wall outside the dormitories. "Nice knowing you, Candace."

"Sure." I rolled my eyes, then started to carry my boxes up the steps. I was in such a rush that I hadn't exactly packed the boxes correctly. As I tilted them, brochures began to spill out, followed by key chains. A sudden breeze blew the brochures in several different directions. I bit back a few curse words as I tried to catch them and in the process spilled the remainder of the key chains.

The moment I saw his shoe on a pile of brochures, my stomach lurched.

"Can I help you now?"

"No one's stopping you." I huffed as I tugged the brochures out from under his foot.

He ran across the courtyard to gather a few that had blown far away. As he walked back, he scooped up key chains as well.

"If you had just let me help you in the first place, this wouldn't have happened, you know."

"Can't you see that just your existence is ruining my life?" I stared at him as he picked up the boxes.

"That's a bit dramatic, don't you think? You spend most of your time in the library anyway. What does it matter if you get a weekend detention there?"

"How do you know that?" I took a slight step back as he brushed past me to carry the boxes into the common room.

"We'd better hurry, our time is almost up." He grabbed me by the elbow and steered me in the direction of the library.

"Wait!" I pulled my arm free. "How do you know I spend so much time in the library? How did you know my name last night?"

"You don't know mine?" He glanced over his shoulder at me. "Let's go, or you're going to make things worse on yourself."

"Of course I know your name. Everyone knows yours." I frowned as I followed after him. "Hardly anyone knows my name."

"Maybe you just don't lift your nose out of a book long enough to realize that some people do." He pulled open the door to the library and held it for me. "Let's go, troublemaker."

"Don't even!" I sighed as I pushed past him.

Ms. Lauren stood in the middle of the library, her arms crossed and her eyes focused on her watch.

"You two made it just in time. I've set up a space for you." She gestured to two desks at the back of the library. "I'd like you to sit there until I tell you that you can leave. If at any time you'd like to confess to me about what happened to the statue, I'll be all ears."

Nicholas didn't say a word as he walked over to one of the desks.

I trudged forward after him, but Ms. Lauren caught me by the shoulder.

"Candace, I'm really surprised at your behavior." She searched my eyes as she lowered her voice. "Did he do something to you? Did he threaten you?"

I thought for a second about answering her truthfully. I could tell her that I felt intimidated by him the night before. I could explain that I didn't want to invite trouble from someone with his reputation. But a small part of me also just didn't want to tell.

I had no idea why I didn't want to tell her the truth. He had destroyed a piece of art. He'd been rude to me. I had plenty of reason to turn him in.

I glanced over at Nicholas, who stared straight at me from his desk. Then I looked back at Ms. Lauren.

"I'm sorry, I don't have anything to say. I've told you that before. I don't know why you don't believe me."

"Candace, I'm extremely disappointed in you." Ms. Lauren marched over to a table and settled into one of the chairs. As she flipped her laptop open, I could sense the anger in her sharp gestures.

I turned back to Nicholas, but his attention had turned to the desk in front of him. As I walked over, he kept his eyes

27

fixated there. I sat down at the desk beside his and sighed. This was certainly not how I'd planned to spend my day.

I glanced over at Nicholas again. Would he try to speak to me? Would he explain how he knew my name—and my habits?

After a few seconds, I realized that he didn't even want to look at me. I sank down in my desk and closed my eyes. I'd sacrificed my Saturday and he couldn't even bother to look at me. Maybe I really was being foolish.

My phone buzzed in my pocket. I gulped and looked toward Ms. Lauren. Had she heard it?

Her focus remained on her laptop. I relaxed. Then my phone buzzed again. Annoyed, I pulled it out of my pocket, intending to silence it. But the message that showed on my screen was from an unknown number.

I DIDN'T KNOW you were so brave.

MY CHEEKS WARMED at the text. No one had ever called me brave before. I studied the phone number. It had to be a friend of mine. I didn't just hand out my number to anyone. But who?

"Better put that away, the boss is headed this way." Nicholas cleared his throat.

I took a sharp breath and shoved the phone back into my pocket.

"I'm going to leave for a short time. I expect you both to sit here quietly. If you do anything other than that, the library staff will report it to me." Her eyes lingered on me. "Behave."

She turned and walked away.

"Behave, Candace," Nicholas muttered and offered me a sly smile.

"Sh." I frowned.

"The librarian is practically deaf, you know that, right?" He stared at me. "Don't you?"

"Yes." I frowned. "Why do you know so much about me?"

"I like to keep tabs on the people that might turn me in." He shrugged. "It's the best way to stay safe."

"Or you could just not do the things that get you in trouble." I glared at him.

"Whatever." He looked back down at his desk.

A few minutes slipped by. I wiggled my toes in my shoes. I thought about the text I'd received. I tried to distract myself by imagining some handsome boy walking through the door, determined to rescue me. Then finally I gave up.

"So why did you do it?" I turned to look at him.

"Huh?" He raised an eyebrow. "Oh, are you talking to me? A lowly criminal?"

"Just tell me the truth." I narrowed my eyes. "You said something about there being a difference between art and brainwashing. So, what is that even supposed to mean? You destroyed something precious all because you want to look tough! That's so pathetic."

"Wow, I'm a criminal and pathetic." He shook his head. "Didn't anyone ever teach you that line...about if you don't have something nice to say?"

"I deserve an answer." I crossed my arms.

SIX

"Oh, do you?" He tipped his head back as he looked at me. A few of his dark curls slid back away from his brown eyes. "What makes you think you deserve an answer?"

"I'm covering for you, aren't I?"

"Or are you just scared?" He leaned forward suddenly, his eyes locked to mine. "What do you think I might do to you, Candace?"

I jumped at his sudden closeness. "Don't do that." I frowned as I slid back in my chair.

"Why?" He continued to study me, though his tone softened. "Isn't that why you haven't said anything to Ms. Lauren? Because you think I'll do something to hurt you? You don't even know me, but you think I'm a monster."

"It's not like there aren't rumors about you." I forced myself to meet his eyes. "You've earned your reputation. Are you going to tell me all those stories are lies?"

"No." He sighed and sat back in his chair. "Some of them are, but not all of them."

Silence settled between us, thick enough for me to slice it. I shifted in my chair and tried to ignore my urge to speak to him again. I shouldn't bother saying a word to him. He was the one who had gotten me into this mess. So why did I feel such a desire to dig deeper?

Maybe because he'd accused me of judging him, without knowing him. I didn't like it when people did that to me. Was it wrong for me to do the same to him?

I stole a look in his direction and found him looking right at me.

"Stop that!" I rolled my eyes.

"What?"

"Looking at me."

"Oh, so now you want to own my eyes too?" He batted his long dark lashes. "What would you do with them if they belonged to you? Would you keep them shut like you do your own?"

"There it is again." I glared at him. "You keep accusing me of being ignorant, but you won't tell me why. You act like you're so superior, but you haven't said a single thing that backs that up."

"I don't have to prove anything to you." He shrugged.

"I'm not asking you to. I'm asking you to stop judging me, the same way you just asked me not to judge you."

"I don't remember asking that."

"Ugh!" I threw my hands in the air. "You are so infuriating!"

"Sh!" The librarian stood up from behind her desk and put her finger to her lips.

"Good job." Nicholas smirked. "You managed to get loud enough to wake her up."

"Sorry." I closed my eyes as I sank down in my chair. Maybe if I just pretended to sleep, he would forget that I was there.

Minutes slipped by.

I opened my eyes just enough to peek at him.

"You're doing it again."

"My eyes are my eyes." He smiled.

"Unbelievable." I sighed.

"What if I did tell you?" He placed his hand on my desk and looked into my eyes. "Would you even bother to listen?"

"Of course, I would listen. I have ears, don't I?"

"Hearing isn't the same thing as listening. You can hear every word I say. That doesn't mean that you'll pay attention and actually think about what I'm saying."

"If it's worth listening to, then I'll listen."

"I'm not sure if I believe you."

"I don't have anything to prove to you." I crossed my arms and locked my eyes to his. "We're stuck here, aren't we? We might as well pass the time with conversation. You don't have to like me, I don't have to like you, but we can still talk."

"I guess you're right about that." He stretched his legs out in front of him and slid down some in his desk. "The truth is, I've been wanting to talk to you for a while."

"Why?"

"Because I don't think your eyes are as closed as the rest of them."

"Okay?" I quirked an eyebrow. "Can you tell me what you're talking about?"

"The statues in the courtyard—they don't apply to everyone, you know."

"What do you mean? They represent what the school stands for. That's all."

"An angel represents purity. It represents an impossible-to-achieve goal. It pressures every student that walks past it to be something that humans simply aren't capable of being." He spread his hands out in front of him. "Not to mention it's a religious symbol and has no business being present at a nondenominational school."

"Is that really why you did it?" I stared at him. "Out of some kind of philosophical outrage?"

"Maybe." He shrugged. "Do you think I'm not capable of philosophical outrage?"

"I don't know." I studied him. "I have no idea what you're capable of, actually. I'm not sure that I want to find out."

"Still scared?" He trailed a fingertip across my desk toward me. "Do you think I might bite you?"

"I think you want me to be." I stared hard at him. "But I'm not."

"Not even a little?" He tapped his fingertip lightly against the desk right in front of me. "Don't you think big bad Nicholas might come after you?"

"I think Nicholas gets a little too much excitement from thinking that he scares people." I smiled. "Your ego is showing."

"My ego, huh?" He grinned. "So, you've been looking at my ego?"

I couldn't help but laugh. As soon as I did, I regretted it. How could I laugh at him? After everything that he'd put me through.

"Careful. Your sense of humor is showing." He drew his hand back, then tilted his head toward the entrance of the library. "Ms. Lauren is back." He put his finger to his lips.

Something about the gesture left me mesmerized.

I ignored the sensation and focused instead on Ms. Lauren's approach.

"I hope you've had enough time to think things through. Are you ready to come clean, Candace?"

"She's got nothing to say to you. Didn't you hear her before?" Nicholas stood up from his desk, his tone sharp.

"Easy, Nicholas." Ms. Lauren glared at him. "I wasn't speaking to you."

"Well, you're going to. You're going to speak to me and only me."

I held my breath as I watched the tension grow between the two.

"Nicholas, maybe we need to discuss this with the principal." Ms. Lauren crossed her arms. "I'll see you both back here for another session of weekend detention tomorrow."

"No, you won't." Nicholas stepped in front of his desk. "I did it. I damaged the statue. Candace has nothing to do with any of this. Alright?"

My eyes widened as I heard him confess. Why would he do that?

"This is it, Nicholas. This is really it this time. You've pushed things too far." She pointed toward the door of the library. "Let's go, we're going straight to the principal about this."

"Relax." He ran his hand back through his hair. "I don't think he's going to be in any hurry to find out what you're doing in your spare time."

"Excuse me?" She glared at him.

"Excuse me, Ms. Lauren, but I'm fairly certain a teacher involved in the kind of recreational writing that you're involved in would be in a good bit of danger of losing her job." He glanced over at me. "Fragile minds and all. I mean, you certainly wouldn't want to be a bad influence on these impressionable young girls, would you?"

"Unbelievable." She scowled. "How could you possibly know about that?"

"I make it my business to know." He locked his eyes to hers. "The question is, does the principal need to know? Does he need to know about any of this? Or can we all just move on?"

"Get out of my sight. Now. Before I change my mind." She pointed to the door again.

"Gladly." He glanced back at me, smiled, then took off out the door.

SEVEN

I stared, shell-shocked, at Ms. Lauren. Exactly what was she writing?

"You're free to go too." She frowned. "I do hope you can be as good at keeping my secret as you were at keeping his."

"Of course." I stood up from the desk and continued to stare at her.

"Just go." She sighed. "Whatever you do, stay away from that guy, alright?"

"I intend to." I spoke the words, but my mind spun with curiosity. How had he gotten information about Ms. Lauren? Did he have it the whole time? If so, why had we spent hours in detention together before he decided to use it?

As I walked across the courtyard, I noticed that all the tables and booths had been packed up. No, I hadn't done anything to save the rain forest—save for the donations that Nicholas made —but I had certainly gotten myself into a bit of a mess.

Nicholas might never speak to me again, but now, I couldn't wait to find out more about him. Something about his confidence—his determination—fascinated me. His words about the angel statue echoed through my mind.

Was he right? Were the statues meant to pressure students into aspiring to goals that were impossible to reach? The thought left me uneasy.

In my opinion, it still didn't excuse his destruction, but it did make him just a little more interesting.

With my heart in my throat, I made my way back to my dorm room. When I stepped inside, I found Apple dancing around the living room with her earbuds in. She spun around and nearly bumped into me as she flung an arm through the air.

"Oops! I'm so sorry!" Apple tugged the earbuds out of her ears.

"It's okay." I smiled as I slipped past her and sat down on the sofa.

"Where were you?" She met my eyes. "I went to the courtyard to find you. You and your table were gone."

"Oh, it's been a crazy day." I rested my head against the sofa cushion and closed my eyes.

"Tell me about it." Apple dropped down beside me.

"I don't even know where to start." I took a deep breath. "Somehow I got tangled up with Nicholas Holden."

"Wait, what?" Apple's eyes widened. "*The* Nicholas Holden? How in the world did you get mixed up with him?"

"Honestly, I'm still not sure." I shook my head. "But, mixed up with him I am."

"How so?"

"I had weekend detention with him."

"What?" She laughed. "Now I know that you're lying. You would never get any kind of detention."

"I did." I stood up and walked over to the kitchen. "Do you know anything about him?"

"Not really. Not anything more than what the rumors are— that he's always in trouble, but he always manages to get out if it."

"But why is he always in trouble? Isn't there some kind of backstory on him? Has he had a hard life or something?" I poured myself a glass of water.

"Oh, wounded puppy syndrome?" Apple smiled. "I don't think that applies to Nicholas. He's more likely to eat the puppy than be the puppy."

"Oh please, he wouldn't eat the puppy." I took a sip of my water.

"Okay, maybe not a puppy, but certainly other cute animals." She giggled, then her smile faded. "I'm sorry, I didn't realize you were serious about this. Candace, he's bad news. That's all you need to know."

"He can't be that bad if he's here at Oak Brook." I shrugged. "It's not like this school is full of gangsters and felons."

"Uh—yes, it is." Apple stared at me. "It's just that most of the gangsters and felons that go here have parents that can pay off the courts. I mean, haven't you been paying attention in class?"

"Apple, it's not that bad." I frowned.

"If it was, we wouldn't know, would we?" She looked into my eyes. "Candy, the important part is that you stay away from him."

"What if I don't want to?" I took another sip of my water.

"Then you need to have your head examined." She shook her head. "Look, I know that it has to be hard to be single while the rest of us are pairing up, but trust me, he's not the guy for you."

"I'm not even considering that!" I held my hands up. "Just forget I said anything, okay? I was just curious about whether you knew anything about him."

"Sorry, I don't." Apple tipped her head toward the door. "Ready to go to dinner?"

"Yes, actually, I'm starving. All I've had to eat all day is that one granola bar."

"Let's go eat. If you really want to know more about Nicholas, you should ask Wes."

"Wes? How does he know anything about Nicholas?"

"I guess they bonded when Wes first arrived. I don't know the whole story, but he might know more than I do." She looped her arm around mine. "I'm sorry I overreacted. I was just surprised that you asked about him."

"It's okay. I kind of surprised myself." I frowned as I tried to ignore the bolt of excitement that carried through me at the thought of finding out more about Nicholas.

When I entered the cafeteria, I couldn't deny the fact that I looked for him. He wasn't sitting at any of the tables.

"There's Wes." Apple pointed him out at our usual table.

I smiled at the others and sat down across from Wes. "Hi, Wes."

"Hi." He looked up from his plate at me, his eyes slightly narrowed.

"What?" I raised an eyebrow.

"Detention?" He stabbed his spaghetti, then swirled it around his fork.

"You heard about that?"

"We all did." Maby leaned across the table to get a good look at me. "Are you sick? Do you need to go to the hospital?"

"Stop it!" I laughed. "I'm not sick. I'm fine."

"I heard that she was covering for someone." Fifi nudged Wes's shoulder. "A guy."

My cheeks flushed as all my friends turned their attention on me. I tended to be the one sitting on the sidelines, listening to other people's stories about their adventures. Now, being in the spotlight, I realized I didn't like it much.

"It was just a misunderstanding." I picked up my fork. "I'm starving." I shoved some spaghetti in my mouth.

"Seems that way." Wes grinned.

Once I'd chewed up the huge bite of spaghetti I'd crammed in my mouth, I looked at Wes.

"What can you tell me about Nicholas Holden?"

"Why do you want to know?" He brushed his hair back from his eyes as he stared at me.

"I'm just curious. Everyone seems to think he's such a bad guy, but why is that? Has he really done terrible things?"

"That depends on what you consider terrible."

"Just tell her yes." Maby spoke up. "He's not a good person, Candy, and you need to stay away from him."

"How bad can he be?" I frowned as I recalled the way he'd spoken up in the library. Was that only because he already knew he had something on Ms. Lauren or had he been trying to protect me?

"Does it matter?" Lala shook her head. "If we're all saying stay away and we're your friends, shouldn't you just listen?"

"I'm just asking a question, it's not as if I'm interested in him." I shivered at the thought.

As I left the cafeteria after dinner, I still wondered about him. If he didn't eat dinner with everyone else, where did he eat dinner? Did he sneak out through the opening in the fence again?

Curious, I decided to check out the area.

The sun began to set as I reached the opening. Other than a few tufts of material caught in the cut chain link fence, there was no sign that anyone had been there. I lingered there for a few more moments —why, I couldn't be sure. What was it about him that drew me in?

I leaned against the fence and thought about the picture I'd taken of him. When I'd seen his face, I'd thought two things.

One, I was in a lot of trouble dealing with Nicholas Holden. Two, he actually looked a little frightened.

As I straightened up and started to walk toward the hideout my friends and I shared, my phone buzzed.

I glanced down at the message on the screen.

YOU SHOULDN'T SPEND SO much time alone.

EIGHT

The words sent a shiver up my spine. Who was this stranger texting me? Was he watching me? I spun around quickly in search of anyone nearby. Nothing moved. Even the wind refused to ruffle my hair. Annoyed, I typed a text back.

I GUESS I'm not alone if you can see me. Stop texting me, creep!

AS SOON AS I sent the text, a part of me regretted it. The first text had been kind and complimentary. What if I really did have a secret admirer?

A second later another text came through.

I'D TALK to you face to face, but I don't think that you can see me.

I HUFFED and shoved my phone into my pocket. Clearly, I'd

43

attracted the attention of a nutcase. All of a sudden, I realized exactly who it was sending me texts. I called the number that texted me and listened as it rang.

I heard the sharp ring of a cell phone, followed by a muttered curse and scuffle behind one of the nearby statues.

"I knew it!" My heart pounded as I marched in the direction of the sounds. "Nicholas Holden! Why are you harassing me?!" I glared at him as he edged out from behind the statue. "Isn't it enough that you got me into trouble? You have to mess with my head too?"

"Candace, if you'll give me a chance to explain..." He reached his hand out toward me.

"Cut it out!" I took a step back out of his reach. "I don't know what kind of weird game you're playing, but I don't want any part of it. Do you understand me? I can't believe I ever doubted my friends. They told me that you're a bad person and I didn't want to believe it. But apparently you enjoy scaring random girls to death!"

"Stop, please!" He frowned and held up his hands. "I didn't mean to scare you. I mean, that's not why I was texting you."

"Sure." I crossed my arms. "What other reason could you possibly have? Oh! I remember now! It was when you took my phone from me. You must have taken my number off of my phone then. Sick." I shook my head. "You'll be lucky if I don't report you to the police."

"Fine, do what you have to." His cheeks reddened as he looked away from me. "I won't bother you again, alright? It was stupid."

"It was more than stupid. It was ridiculous." I scowled at him. "Don't you have better things to do with your time? Like breaking and entering? Or assault?"

"I guess I have fallen behind on my criminal acts lately." He shoved his hands into his pockets. "I've been a little distracted."

"Poor thing. Has someone been harassing you and trying to ruin your life?" I forced back a sudden rush of tears as I turned away from him. "I guess I make an easy enough target, right? The pathetic girl that spends too much time alone. Sure, she'd be easy enough to torture. Why not give it a go?"

"Candace."

His voice sounded closer, but I refused to look in his direction to find out how close he was.

"Is that what you think I was doing?" His voice softened. "I'm sorry. I'm sorry I ever spoke to you in the first place. I never wanted to hurt you."

"Yeah, right." I wiped at my eyes before too many tears could fall. I wouldn't give him the satisfaction of seeing me cry. "Just go back to whatever hole you live in and leave me alone, alright?"

"I will." His voice was just beside me now.

I held my breath as I felt his fingertips on the curve of my elbow. Did he intend to hurt me?

I knew I should be frightened, but for some strange reason I wasn't. In fact, I felt that strange bolt of electricity again. I'd felt it before, when our hands had brushed against each other. I told myself to pull away, but it didn't hurt when his touch coasted along my bare skin. Instead, it felt incredibly soothing.

"Nicholas." I met his eyes, despite my better judgment.

"I'm sorry." He looked straight into my eyes, his voice still gentle. "It was stupid, I know it was. I don't have a lot of experience with these kinds of things. I thought if tried to talk to you face to face about it, you wouldn't give me a chance. I mean, how could someone like you give someone like me a chance?"

"What are you talking about?" I could barely breathe as his palm curved along my elbow and down toward my wrist.

"I wasn't trying to terrorize you, Candace. I just didn't know how to tell you how I felt. Especially after what you saw. I knew then that you wouldn't want anything to do with me. But then I got to spend some time with you and you weren't cruel like other people are. You seemed to be interested in what I had to say. So, I thought maybe there was a chance. I was an idiot and I'm sorry. I never meant to frighten you. I promise, I won't text you again. I won't even look at you." He pulled his hand away and frowned. "I knew better. I just took a stupid chance."

"Nicholas, are you trying to tell me that you texted me because you like me?" I stared at him.

"Yes." He stared back at me.

"Like like me?"

"I know, it's crazy." He licked his lips. "I tried not to think about it, but then everywhere I looked, you were there, and I just couldn't get you out of my head."

"This is a joke, isn't it?" I rolled my eyes. "You're just trying to prank me. What? Are your buddies hiding out around here somewhere ready to jump out and laugh at me?"

"It's not a joke." His voice sharpened, then he took a breath. "Look, I don't expect you to understand, alright? I'll get over it. Like I said, I won't text you anymore. I'll stay out of your way." He turned and walked off toward the opening in the fence.

Shocked, my voice stuck in my throat. My thoughts refused to form full sentences. How? Why? Was it possible?

My heartbeat quickened and to my surprise that urge I'd had to know more about him turned into a desperate need to stop him from walking away. My hand wrapped around his just before he could duck through the fence.

"Nicholas, wait." My mind buzzed as my fingers tightened around his. How could I be touching him like this? My thoughts swam with all the warnings from my friends, with the memory of him destroying the statue, with that smug smirk on his lips when he'd teased me.

"What?" He turned back to face me, his hand loose and

warm in mine. He stared into my eyes. "Do you have something to say, Candace? Or do you only want to tell me more about what your friends think of me?"

This wasn't a joke. This was real. Nicholas Holden, the baddest of all the bad boys at Oak Brook Academy had a crush on me?

"I don't know what to say."

"I just wanted a chance." He started to pull his hand free. "It was a stupid idea."

"Don't go." I tightened my grip on his hand.

"That's what you have to say?" He whispered his words as he shifted closer to me. "You want me to stay?"

NINE

My heart skipped a beat as he stared at me, waiting for an answer. How could I answer him when I had no idea how I actually felt? Sure, I'd gotten curious. I wanted to know more about him. I felt strange around him. But did that mean that I was actually interested in him?

"So, do you want me to stay?"

"I don't know." I took a sharp breath as the words slipped out of my mouth.

"Okay, then you can come with me." He tugged me forward, toward the opening in the fence.

"What?" My eyes widened. "I don't have permission to leave the grounds."

"When you go this way, you don't need permission." He flashed a smile in my direction. "Let's go. There's a place I want to show you."

Maybe I could overlook Nicholas's questionable behavior within the safety of the grounds of Oak Brook, but to go with him out into the city at night? I had no idea what places he might want to show me, but I doubted that they were places I wanted to see.

"Scared?" He trailed his thumb across the back of my hand and gave my fingers a light squeeze. "You've got to decide sometime, Candace. It might as well be now."

"Decide what?" I tried to ignore the tingling that his caress inspired in my hand.

"Decide whether I'm a bad guy. Whether I'm dangerous." His gaze lingered on mine. "It's now or never, right?"

"I don't do things like this." I shifted from one foot to the other. "I don't get detention, I don't sneak off campus, I don't wander through the city with strangers at night."

"I'm not that much of a stranger." He shrugged. "We've been going to school together for a while now. Just because you never noticed me, doesn't mean I never noticed you."

"It's not that I didn't notice you."

"You just didn't look past the surface, right?" He tipped his head to the side and that curl of hair tickled across his eyebrow. "Don't worry, I don't blame you. I work hard to make sure people look away. This isn't easy for me either, you know." He took a deep breath. "I don't usually ask for company."

I knew that I shouldn't. I knew that I should just turn around and march right back to my dorm room. I could tell Apple all about it and we could eat snacks and watch a good romance movie. I could forget all about this strange encounter and return to my normal life.

My normal boring life.

Making the right choice hadn't led to anything worthwhile so far in my life. I'd been the best child I could be and my parents were still taken from me. I'd been the best granddaughter I could be and my grandmother still got sick and needed me to take care of her. I'd tried more than once to be the best girlfriend I could be and it always ended up in disaster. What if just once I made the wrong choice?

As I stared into his warm brown eyes, I was certain that he

was the wrong choice. Not just because of his reputation, but because he coaxed me toward breaking rules and taking risks. Everything I'd ever learned from movies and television shows warned me that these types of things led down the wrong path in life.

He pulled his hand from mine.

My heart lurched.

He shook his head. "Never mind. I don't want to make you do anything that you don't want to do." He ruffled his hand through his hair. "This was a bad idea from the beginning. Honestly, I'm usually way smoother than this. Something about you makes me stumble and trip over my words. I guess that's why I haven't been able to look away." He shrugged. "But that's my problem, isn't it? Not yours. You're right. You shouldn't leave campus. You shouldn't break the rules." He looked down at his scuffed boots. "And you certainly shouldn't trust a stranger like me."

I pushed past him before I could think of a word to say. I knew that if I didn't follow through in that second, I wouldn't do it. He had sent me that text during detention; he'd called me brave. I wanted to be brave. Not to impress him, but because I was so tired of being frightened, of waiting, of holding my breath while the world continued to spin around me.

"Let's go." I glanced back at him.

He stared at me with wide eyes. "Are you sure?"

"Do you want me to change my mind?"

"No." He laughed as he swept his arm around me and pulled me toward the sidewalk in the distance. "Hurry, there are cameras up here."

At the mention of cameras, my heartbeat quickened again. Instantly I regretted my choice. I didn't have anything to black-mail teachers with. I didn't know how to talk my way out of trouble like Nicholas did. How could I do something so stupid?

"Hurry, Candace!" He grinned as he laced his fingers through mine and ran down the sidewalk.

I broke into a run to keep up with him. As I sucked down the night air and my lungs grew tight from a mixture of nervousness and exertion, I became aware of the wind blowing through my hair. I felt a part of my heart open up that I didn't know had been locked away.

I laughed and ran faster until he had to keep up with me. I tugged him forward, ignoring the crowds of people on the sidewalk and the blaring sounds of the traffic. I kept running, even though I had no idea where I was going. I ran until I thought my heart might burst.

"Candace!" Nicholas panted as he tugged at my hand. "Slow down!"

I lurched forward and rested my hands on my knees as I sucked in hungry breaths of air.

He pulled my hair back from where it hung in my face and tucked it behind my ear. "You okay?"

I looked into his eyes as I continued to try to catch my breath. Even if I could have spoken, I had no idea what I would say. Claiming to be okay certainly didn't cover it. I felt strange and wild and more different than I'd ever felt in my entire life. I realized, as he stared back at me, that he probably thought I'd lost my mind.

"Wow, you're beautiful." He curved his hand under my chin and gazed into my eyes.

Mesmerized by the heat in his eyes, I couldn't move for a moment. I knew that I should speak, but no words came to mind. Had he really just said that?

A horn blared not far from us and jarred me out of my dazed state. I pulled back from his touch and straightened up.

"This was a mistake." I took a step away from him.

"No." He caught my hand. "It wasn't."

"It was." My head spun as my heart pounded. "This isn't me. This isn't who I am."

"Maybe it is." He murmured his words as he stepped closer to me. "Maybe you've just never let yourself be free."

"Free?" I stared hard into his eyes. "What does free mean to you? That you get to dazzle me, feed me superficial lines, and take advantage of my ignorance?"

"It's not like that."

"It's exactly like that." I closed my eyes, then shook my head. "I fell for it, didn't I?"

"Is that what you want to think?"

"Just be real with me, Nicholas." I looked straight at him. "How many girls have you pulled this same scam with?"

He licked his lips, took a step back, then trailed his fingertips back through his hair. He looked out into the traffic, then back at me.

"A few."

TEN

"A few." I nodded, then turned to walk away.

"Wait." He stepped in front of me and tried to meet my eyes. "Listen, I'm no angel. I never claimed to be, remember?"

"Just stop, please." I tried to ignore the throbbing pain that coursed through my head. "You've made enough of a fool out of me."

"Okay, look." He continued to walk backwards a few steps in front of me. "I just wanted to show you something. I don't want you wandering around the city by yourself. Come with me, I'll show you what I want to show you and then I'll take you back to Oak Brook. No pressure, no games."

"I'm not sure that you're capable of that."

"I know you want me to pull back the curtain and reveal a prince." He brushed his curls back from his eyes. "But this is all you get Candace—a frog. But this frog knows of the most beautiful spot in New York City and you look like a princess that needs to see it."

"Don't call me that."

"Princess?" He smirked. "That's what you are, isn't it?"

"Not even close." I crossed my arms.

"Hey, I'll call you whatever you want—if you give me a chance." He stared at me. "Believe me or don't, but there's something about you. I can't explain it. I'd like to figure it out. Wouldn't you?"

"Maybe." I sighed. I couldn't deny that despite my anger at him and his ruse, I still felt intrigued by him.

"Let's go." He held his hand out to me. "You won't regret it, I promise."

"I'm not going anywhere with you." I glared at him.

"Why not?" He let his hand fall back to his side, but his eyes locked to mine. "It hasn't been too bad so far, has it? I saw the way you ran. Have you ever felt anything like that before?" He took a step closer to me.

My heart still pounded with the adrenaline I'd felt. It wasn't just from the run, it was from breaking the rules, from doing what I wanted without giving thought to the consequences. Also, the thrill of having him pursue me, notice me, take an interest in me. That was the part that left me feeling uneasy.

I remembered the warnings my friends gave me not long before. What was it about him that made me ignore common sense?

"You must really think you're some kind of Casanova, huh?" I shook my head. "I'm not going to fall for it."

"I'm not trying to convince you of anything. I saw it in your eyes when you ran. You know what you felt and you know that you have me to thank for that." He held his hands out in both directions. "I'll take you back to Oak Brook right now. But I know that's not what you really want. So either suck it up and face the fact that you're not the straight-laced little soldier that you've always been told you are, or tell me right now that you'd rather be holed up in your dorm room listening to your friend drivel on about her boyfriend instead of being right here, right now, with me."

I hated him for more than one reason. I hated him because he'd made me think for just a second that there might be something real between us. I hated him for witnessing one of the most primal experiences I'd ever had. I hated him for the stupid curls that kept falling into his eyes and the curve of his full lips. But most of all, I hated him because he was right.

My heart raced at the thought of exploring the city with him. It sank when I considered the option of going back to my dorm room. I loved Apple and I was happy that she had found someone she adored. But I didn't think I could stomach one more conversation about her love life.

It wasn't really his fault that I'd let myself get caught up in the idea of having something real with him. That was the fault of the romantic movies I watched, of my friends finding their own timeless loves, of me always hoping that there would be one special someone.

But maybe that was the problem. Just like I'd always followed the rules when it came to life, I'd always followed the rules when it came to love too. I picked boys that weren't too different, weren't too daring, and certainly weren't too wild. But I'd never felt like this with any of them. I'd never felt this before at all.

I had Nicholas to thank for that. Maybe he wasn't that one special someone, but he was someone who had awakened something in me. Was that such a terrible thing?

"Okay." I took a deep breath and held out my hand to him. "I will stay with you—as your friend."

"My friend?" He took my hand, then smiled. "Am I supposed to shake it? Is this some kind of business deal?"

"I don't want to be your prey." I met his eyes. "I don't want to be conned. I just want to enjoy this a little bit. I want to see what it's like to have some fun."

"My prey?" He dropped his hand back to his side. A flicker

of anger darkened his eyes. "Just what kind of rumors have you heard about me?"

"It doesn't matter. Tonight, can we just be two people? Not students at Oak Brook, not Nicholas with the bad reputation, not Candace with no reputation at all, but just two people?" I watched the anger fade from his expression. "I just want to be here with you, not whoever you think you have to be. I'm never going to be convinced to be anything more than your friend, but if that's enough for you, then I'd like to be that."

"Never, huh?"

"Never." I stared into his eyes and ignored the skip of my heartbeat. It didn't matter what my body said when he looked at me with those warm eyes and that faint smirk. It didn't matter that I was more curious about him than I'd ever been about any of my friends. All that mattered was that I had decided there would never be anything between us. "So should I stay?"

"Yes." He reached his hand out to me. "Just us, best of pals."

"Just us." I smiled as I shook his hand.

"Now, let's go." He kept his hand wrapped around mine and tugged me forward. "I still have something to show you."

As I ran forward, pulled along by his determination, I allowed myself to relax. This could be a very good night. I'd already learned a lot about myself. Now that the boundaries were clear between us, I wouldn't have to worry about him pushing for more. If only my hand would stop tingling in his grasp and my mind would stop spinning when he glanced back to check on me, I'd be just fine.

Just friends, I reminded myself. That's all we'll ever be. He's not the type to have a girlfriend, to treat her the way a good boyfriend should. He's not the type to be trusted.

"Almost there." He laughed as he slowed down. "I didn't think you'd be able to keep up."

"I can keep up just fine." I grinned. "So, are you going to tell me where we're going now?"

"I don't have to tell you." He smiled as he gestured to the bridge that stretched out before us. "I can show you. We're already here."

"The Brooklyn Bridge?" I stopped on the sidewalk and stared at the massive bridge stretched out before me. Sure, it was a sight to see. It stretched across the water with a sense of magnificence that few other bridges could muster. But it was just the Brooklyn Bridge.

"You really think I've never seen this before?"

"Not with me you haven't." He offered me his hand. "Let me show you."

ELEVEN

I stared at his hand for a long moment. I knew what would happen when I took it. He'd take off running and I'd have no idea what his intentions were.

"I can get there just fine on my own, thanks."

"If that's what you prefer." He fell into step beside me. "But I have a feeling before this night is over, you're going to be holding onto me real tight."

"No, that's not a feeling. That's a fantasy." I brushed my hair back over my shoulder, then quickened my pace. "We've already put all that behind us, remember?"

"Maybe you have, but it's right in front of me." He smirked as I glanced back at him.

"You really think you're clever, don't you?"

"You think I am, don't you?"

"I can't believe your idea of a wild night is to walk across the Brooklyn Bridge." I looked out over the railing. "It's beautiful, there's no question about that. But it's not exactly what I expected."

"No sex, drugs, or rock and roll?" He smiled as he leaned against the railing beside me. "See, the part that I left out is that we're going to be bungee jumping off the Brooklyn Bridge. That's a bit more my speed, right?"

"What?" I turned to look at him. "There's no way I'm doing that."

"Don't worry, I won't let you fall." He flicked a few strands of my hair back from my cheek. "Promise."

"Not a chance." My eyes widened. "Is that even a thing that people can do? I mean, did you bring your own bungee cord? Do you know how dangerous that is?"

"Take a breath." He laughed, his eyes dancing as he looked at me. "It was a joke, just a joke."

"See, that's the problem." I shook my head. "I can never tell when you're being serious or when you're joking."

"If you get to know me better, you might be able to tell." He tipped his head toward the walkway. "This isn't exactly what I wanted to show you. Follow me." He tucked his hands into his pockets. "No hand holding required."

Intrigued, I followed after him. He continued along the walkway until we reached the middle of the bridge. He stopped near one of the tall archways and turned back to face me. "Here we are."

"Where?" I looked over at the water. "It *is* a great view."

"The view is nice, but that's not what I want to show you." He pointed up above him. "We're going up.'

"Up?" I stared at him.

"Right there, see where the spikes are? Just climb them."

A temporary ladder had been constructed leading up to a platform where repair work was underway during the day. At the moment, the large platform was empty. The ladder was nothing more than long spikes that stuck out from a spine bolted to the stone.

"Climb them?" I looked into his eyes. "Have you lost your mind?"

"It's safe. It's used for repairs. As long as you're careful, you'll be just fine." He placed his hand against the small of my back. "I won't let you fall."

"This seems like a terrible idea." I grabbed one of the spikes and looked up at the platform above me.

"Those tend to be the best kind." He gave my back a light pat. "All you have to do is make the choice. You can climb up and see what I promised you or you can go back to Oak Brook and wonder what you missed. I mean, clearly there's a safe choice."

"But it's not always the right choice." I narrowed my eyes.

I began to climb, without exactly deciding to do it. I figured I could go up a little bit, then climb back down if it felt like too much.

As I took my next step, Nicholas mounted the first one. His arms spread across my shoulders as he reached for the spikes just below my grasp.

"Keep going, I'll be right here."

Keep going? His body sprawled across mine made my head spin. I could barely take a breath. But he expected me to climb? I thought about telling him to stop, but the way he enveloped me made me feel safe.

I reached for the next spike and climbed further. He moved with me. I was so dazed by his closeness that I hadn't even noticed how far we'd gone until a gust of wind made me shiver.

"That's it, I want to go back." My body tensed with fear.

"We're already there." His breath tickled along my neck as he spoke. "Look up."

I forced myself to look up and saw the platform right above me. A quick look down proved that I was unnaturally high above the bridge and above the water that coursed beneath it.

Terrified, I wondered how I'd managed to climb so high

without realizing it. It was just supposed to a few steps—to prove that I could do it—not all the way to the top.

"Nicholas, I can't." My voice trembled as I clung to the spikes. "I'm going to fall!"

"I've got you." He tightened his body around mine. I could feel the outline of his chest as it pressed against my back and the warmth of his skin beneath his shirt. "I won't let you fall. Just climb up. I promise you, it's worth it."

"I don't think I can." I bit into my bottom lip.

"I'm right here, I'll be right with you." His lips briefly touched the curve of my neck.

The caress sent lightning through every inch of my body. It was probably an accident. He was holding me so tightly, he had nowhere else to put his lips when he talked. Accident or not, it left me feeling dizzier than looking down at the bridge below.

I took a slow breath and reached for the platform above me.

As I started to climb up onto it, he pressed his hand against the curve of my thigh to give me a boost up onto the platform. It was that touch that reminded me of exactly who he was. His lips against my neck was no accident, he was still trying to con me. He'd admitted to running the same scam on a few other girls. Was I really going to let him get away with it?

I jerked my leg away from his touch and shimmied up onto the platform before he could get his hands anywhere else on me. Driven by my anger, I didn't even realize that I'd made it to safety until he pulled himself up beside me.

"Wow!" He stared at me, his eyes as wide as his smile.

"Wow!" I gasped as I looked out over the water. The view that spread out before me was nothing I'd ever seen before. It was as if the entire city was visible, and beyond that, the water and the outstretched sky. It took my breath away as I drank it all in.

"I know." He sat down beside me. His hand rested near mine but didn't touch it. "Isn't it amazing?"

"It's more than that." I continued to stare out at the view. "It's like nothing I've ever seen before."

"I told you it would be worth it."

"And how many other girls have you told that to?" I glanced over at him.

"A few." He smiled as he met my eyes.

"I guess this is your regular spot then?" I blushed as I recalled how frightened I'd been when I climbed up the spikes. I must have looked ridiculous to him.

"Mine, yes." He shifted a little closer to me. "I like to come up here when I can. It gives me a new perspective on things." He draped his arm across my shoulders. "I can't even see Oak Brook from here. But when I look up, it feels like I can see the entire universe."

"Easy there." I shrugged his arm off my shoulders. "I'm not like all the other girls you bring here."

"No, you're not." He rested his hand against the platform behind me as he looked at me. "You're the first."

"The first?" I laughed. "The first one that didn't fall for your 'arm around the shoulders look into the universe' move?"

A shadow flickered through his eyes as he glanced away. He took a breath, then looked back at me.

"No. You're the first to climb up here with me." He searched my eyes. "I have to admit, I really didn't think you'd be brave enough. But I hoped that you might be."

TWELVE

His words and the way his eyes probed mine, made my resolve grow fainter.

"Is that true?"

"What do you think?" He held my gaze.

"I don't know."

"You do." He slid his hand toward me so that his arm pressed against my back.

"I don't." I looked away but didn't shift away from him. I didn't mind feeling his warmth against me.

"Then you're the liar." He laughed quietly as he looked back up at the sky. "You can believe what you want about me, Candace, but it's not going to change the truth. So, what's it going to be? Believe what everyone else has to say about me or listen to what your heart tells you?"

"What makes you think my heart tells me anything about you?" I sharpened my tone. I couldn't get lost in the way my heart pounded or how handsome he looked with a mixture of city lights and moonlight splayed across his upturned face.

"You're here, aren't you?" He curved his arm around my back—just enough to embrace me—and pressed his hand against the platform beside me. "Nobody does something as crazy as this unless their heart is in it."

I fell silent. I couldn't argue his point. I hadn't climbed the spikes just to prove to him that I could.

I'd climbed them because I wanted to see what he saw. I wanted to know what he considered special.

Logic told me that I wasn't the first girl he'd brought up on this platform. I certainly wasn't the bravest girl at Oak Brook or in all of New York City. So why should I believe him when he said I was the first to climb?

But my heart told me something different. My heart told me that he didn't want to lie to me anymore.

Was it my heart or just wishful thinking? Either way I rested my head against his shoulder and drank in the view. He didn't have to be Nicholas and I didn't have to be Candace. We could just be two people staring into the universe just for one night.

Minutes slid by with neither of us speaking. I noticed that he didn't try to take advantage of my closeness. He could have easily tightened his grasp around me. His hands could have wandered just about anywhere they pleased. He could have tipped his head just enough to try to kiss me. But he didn't. His arm remained around me and his hand remained against the platform.

I could have sat there for hours, just like that. Lost in his warmth and the expanse of the sky.

Then the spotlight hit us.

I jerked back as the bright light struck my eyes.

His arm tightened around me to steady me. "Careful." His sharp tone was full of warning.

"What's happening?" I shielded my eyes as I looked down at the bridge. A police car had pulled off to the side and its spotlight pointed right at us.

"Time to go." His stern voice made my heart pound. "I'll start down first, you come right behind me, okay? Go slow."

"Now?" I took a sharp breath. I hadn't really thought about getting down. I didn't want to think about it. Going up had been scary enough but going down—and straight into the watchful stare of a police officer—left me feeling panicked.

"Candace." He gripped my shoulders and looked into my eyes. "I told you, I've got you. Remember? I'm not going to let you fall. Just go slow and we'll be at the bottom before you know it."

"What about the police officer?"

"Don't worry about him." He smiled. He stretched one leg down off the edge of the platform and climbed down a few of the spikes. Then he paused and gestured for me to come with him.

I trembled as I neared the edge of the platform. Why had I ever climbed up in the first place? How could I make such a foolish choice? I squeezed my eyes shut and eased my foot down to the second spike. Once I felt it solid under my foot, I slid down the next.

Seconds later his body was around mine again as he guided me back down to the bridge. Despite the fear that coursed through me, I still savored the sensation of his closeness. When he dropped down from the last spike, I heard another voice.

"I've warned you about this enough times." The spotlight turned off. A flashlight turned on and flicked from Nicholas to me. "I can't believe you actually got a girl to go up with you this time. Do you know how dangerous what you did is, young lady?' He pointed the flashlight into my face as I turned around to face him.

"I'm sorry, sir." I mumbled my words as I tried to shield my eyes.

"Nico, this has to stop." The police officer shifted the flashlight onto Nicholas's face. "I told you the last time, I'm not going to keep letting you slide."

"It's not hurting anyone." Nicholas scowled at him. "It's just a little fun."

"See, it's your idea of fun that worries me." The officer cleared his throat. "I'm taking you in this time."

"What?" Nicholas narrowed his eyes.

"What?" I gasped as I looked at the police car.

"Both of you." The officer yanked the back door of the police car open. "Maybe it will knock some sense into you. I could have been called out here to scrape you both off the pavement, don't you get that?" He grabbed Nicholas by the arm and shoved him toward the car. "When your father hears about this—"

"No, don't." Nicholas pulled back and stared hard at the officer. "You're not going to tell him."

"That's where you're wrong. I've been doing you too many favors."

"You know what I can tell him about you." Nicholas glared at him.

"I don't care anymore, Nico. My job isn't worth finding you dead somewhere because you're too reckless to be smart. Now get in the car." He gestured to the open door.

I felt as if I was seeing everything from a distance. It all had to be a dream. I couldn't have climbed up the side of a bridge. That police officer wasn't shouting at Nicholas. Nico?

I'd never heard anyone call him that before.

"Just let her go, alright?" Nicholas's tone softened. "She didn't do anything wrong. Whatever grudge you have with me, you don't have to take it out on her."

"Oh no, she's coming with us." He pointed the flashlight at me again. "She needs to get a healthy dose of reality."

"You know you're not supposed to do this. It's against policy." Nicholas crossed his arms. "When my father finds out that you risked exposing me, you're going to be in so much trouble."

"I'd worry more about what your father is going to do when he finds out you were up on the top of that bridge." The officer glared at him. "He and this entire city go to a lot of trouble to protect you and this is how you show your gratitude? Get in the car. It's the last time I'll tell you. Unless you want your girlfriend here to see me throw you against the hood and cuff you. Is that what you want? Trying to look tough to impress her?"

"Stop." Nicholas frowned. He glanced over at me, then sullenly turned back to the car. As he settled into the backseat, he refused to look at me.

"You too." The officer gestured to the door.

I sighed. I realized I'd been holding my breath. I really expected Nicholas to talk his way out of trouble, like he always did. But apparently there was a lot I didn't know about Nicholas, a lot that most people didn't know.

I settled into the seat beside him.

The officer slammed the door closed, then settled into the driver's seat.

My heart sank as he turned his flashing lights and siren on. This was real.

No, he hadn't read me my rights, but I certainly wasn't free to go.

THIRTEEN

Nicholas didn't say a word to me for the entire drive. When we were led out of the police car and into the police station, he refused to look at me.

Didn't he have anything to say? An apology? A promise that he would get us out of this mess?

I could only imagine my grandmother's reaction when she got a call from the police station detailing my crime. She wouldn't believe them. She'd laugh about it. Then she'd think of ways to murder me.

I squirmed as I sat in a chair in front of the officer's desk. Nicholas sat in the chair beside me but kept his focus on the floor.

"I'll be right back. Don't move." The officer walked away from his desk toward a long hallway in the rear of the police station.

I held my breath as I waited for Nicholas's next move. He remained still, silent as ever.

"Well?" I nudged his shoe with mine.

"Well what?" He looked over at me, then looked away quickly.

"You have a plan, right?"

"A plan?" He shook his head. "We're in a police station. What do you think I am, a magician?"

"Oh no." I closed my eyes. "I can't believe this is happening."

"Relax." He frowned. "It's not going to be as bad as you think."

"How does he even know you? Nico?" I stared at him. "Who is your father?"

His jaw tightened, but his lips didn't move.

I opened my mouth to ask him again, but the police officer walked back over before I could.

"You can go." The officer set a cup of coffee down on his desk.

"Great." Nicholas started to stand up.

"No, not you. Her." He tipped his head toward me. "There's a bus down the street that will get you back to Oak Brook."

"A bus? At this time of night?" Nicholas shook his head. "No way, she can't go on the bus."

"Oh, now you're worried about her safety?" The policeman rolled his eyes. "She can call a taxi. I'm sure she's got the funds, right?" He looked over at me.

"I can get back." I nodded and stood up.

"Then go, get out of here, before I change my mind."

"Like any of this is up to you." Nicholas crossed his arms.

I stepped away from the desk, then paused and turned back. "He didn't do anything wrong. I did what I did because I wanted to. It was my choice."

"Well, doesn't that make you the brightest bulb in the box?" The officer shook his head. "Listen to my advice, darling, and stay as far away from this one as you can. You." He pointed at Nicholas. "You're coming with me."

Nicholas turned to look at me as he stood up. His lips parted as if he wanted to say something, then fell closed again. Not a trace of his cocky attitude remained.

I stared at him a moment longer, then turned and walked toward the exit of the police station. What else could I do? Nicholas's bad behavior had caught up with him.

Still, as I stepped outside, a shiver coursed up my spine. Could I really leave him behind? I turned back to the doors and watched as Nicholas was led toward an elevator in the lobby. Not back toward where I guessed the holding cells would be. Not handcuffed.

I pulled out my phone and ordered a taxi. As I waited, I sent a text to exactly who I knew I needed to talk to.

PLEASE MEET me at the hideout. I need to talk to you ASAP.

WHEN THE TAXI PULLED UP, I hesitated again. I should have been angry at him for putting me in these circumstances. I should have been relieved to be away from him and not caught up in the middle of whatever he was involved in.

Instead, the thought of leaving him made my chest ache with dread.

I settled into the back of the taxi and closed my eyes. I'd promised myself that I'd be careful around him, that I could never possibly feel anything more than friendship for him. But as the taxi pulled away and my mind spun with panic, I realized that I'd already broken that promise.

I couldn't recall the single moment that it had happened, but somewhere along the line I'd gone too far. I'd let myself slip from a little harmless fantasy into full-blown feelings.

Not that it mattered. Did someone like Nicholas even have those kinds of feelings?

My stomach twisted with guilt after that thought. I'd looked into his eyes—far behind that smugness, far beyond the confidence that he wore like a mask—and I'd seen a different person.

When I arrived at Oak Brook my heart pounded as I stepped through the gates. Had the police officer called the principal? Would security be waiting for me?

Instead, I was greeted by quiet—a bit more quiet than what I'd expect for a Saturday night—until I glanced at the clock on my phone. Almost one in the morning.

I sighed as I realized I'd also missed curfew.

I'd given up on the idea that anyone would be at the hideout to meet me, when I received a response to my text.

BE RIGHT THERE.

SURPRISED, I headed to the hideout.

The building on the far end of the campus had once been used for classrooms, but when the new buildings were built, the older ones had been designated for storage. The buildings were rarely ever accessed anymore. My friends had found their way in to one of them and made it their own home away from home.

Using the items in storage, we'd decorated the first floor with curtains, lamps, and paintings. The floor was scattered with cushions that we could sprawl out on and the ceiling and walls were covered with murals. It was a safe space in the sometimes high-pressure environment of Oak Brook Academy.

When I stepped inside, I began to pace. I knew that I had to find out the truth, but I wasn't one to demand things. I didn't force people to tell me the truth, but this time, I planned to try my hardest.

"Candy?" Wes stepped through the door. "What's going on? Is everything alright?"

"You tell me." I crossed my arms as I looked at him. "Who is Nicholas Holden?"

"You know who he is." He narrowed his eyes. "Were you out with him again? Apple was looking for you earlier and everyone was worried about you. We all told you to stay away from him."

"And why is that?" I raised an eyebrow. "What is it that you're not telling me?"

"I don't have anything to say about him." He crossed his arms and shook his head.

"I'm sorry, Wes, but that isn't good enough." My heart pounded as I stared into his eyes. Wes and I weren't particularly close and I knew he could have a bit of a temper when pushed. I braced myself for his reaction to my demands.

"I can't tell you." He frowned. "Alright? I found out more than I should have about him and I can't tell you or anyone else."

"Unbelievable. If you were really concerned about my safety, you'd tell me all the details." Frustration boiled up within me. "Why can't you just tell me the truth?"

"Because it's not just about your safety, Candy, it's about his too. Alright?" He stared at me. "I can't tell you, but I have told you that you should keep your distance. Clearly, you didn't listen to anyone's advice. I'm going to tell you one more time—stay away from him. There are plenty of other guys."

"It's not about that!" I glared at him.

"Sure it isn't. It's one in the morning, you disappeared, didn't tell anyone where you were going, and now you're acting like someone I've never met before. But it has nothing to do with being caught up in something. You shouldn't be with someone you never should have looked twice at." He pointed his finger at me. "I warned you, remember that."

"Great, thanks." I rolled my eyes as he left the hideout.

I wanted to shout at him, to insist that he was wrong. But I couldn't. All I could think about was Nicholas in that police station and the great mystery that hung over his head.

Could he really be that bad?

FOURTEEN

The light from my phone emanated through the darkness in my room. I stared at the background and the collection of apps littered across it. Why hadn't he texted me? It had been hours since I'd left him at the police station and I hadn't heard a word from him. Had he really been arrested?

I tried to keep my eyes open, but the exhaustion from my crazy night caused me to doze off.

I woke up hours later with my phone still in my hand.

"Still no text." I winced as I moved my arm, which I'd slept on in a strange position. I knew that I shouldn't care what happened to him. I should only be interested in how to stay away from him after what had happened the night before.

But I just needed to know that he was okay. When I closed my eyes, I could still feel his arms around me, his lips against the curve of my neck. I doubted that I'd ever forget that.

I climbed out of bed, despite the fact that it was barely after five. As I pulled on some clothes, a plan formed in my mind. It was crazier than any plan I'd ever considered. There was no question in my mind that Nicholas had been a bad influence on me so far. I could hear my grandmother's words in my head.

"Your choices are the most important tools you have in your life. Make the right ones and you'll have a better life than I ever did."

I never really understood her message, since she'd had a pretty good life. She had enough money to buy anything she could ever want and she was quite popular and well respected. However, I had seen the sadness in her eyes when she drank her glass of wine in the evening with only me for company.

Her disappointment and wrath was a risk I had to take.

I grabbed a baseball cap and tucked my hair under it. Then I pulled on a plain bulky t-shirt I used to sleep in now and then. I finished the look with a loose pair of jeans and some old sneakers. A quick glance in the mirror revealed I still very much looked like a girl, but I hoped it would be enough.

I headed down the stairs and crossed the common room to the entrance of the boys' dormitory. As I passed by a security guard engrossed in his morning newspaper, I lowered my head and turned my body to the side.

"Morning." The guard coughed.

I cleared my throat, then spoke in the lowest voice I could muster. "Morning." I held my breath as I waited for his reaction.

The pages of his newspaper rustled as he moved on to the next section.

With my heart in my throat I climbed the stairs to the second floor of the boys' dormitory. I'd never been there before. It didn't look much different than the girls' dormitory, but it did smell a little different. Bursts of cologne instead of the flowery scent of perfume hung in the air.

It hadn't taken much research to figure out which dorm room he was in. But would he answer or would his roommate?

I paused in front of the door and looked both ways down the hallway. No one else appeared to be awake. I bit into my bottom lip. Had I become this desperate?

A few strands of my hair popped out from beneath my hat and hit my cheek.

Yes. Clearly, I had.

I squeezed my eyes shut and lifted my hand to knock on the door. I just wanted to be sure that he was okay. That was all I wanted. Then I could move on with my life.

After a few quick knocks, I dropped my hand back to my side and braced myself for what might happen next. With each pound of my heart I wondered if he'd even answer.

A few minutes slid past before I had to decide whether to knock again. Just one more time, I promised myself as I lifted my hand into the air.

Before my knuckles could strike the wood, the door inched open.

I felt eyes on me, then the door jerked all the way open.

"Candace?" He stared at me, his eyes heavy with sleep.

"Not a great disguise, I guess." I tucked my hair back under my hat. My cheeks warmed as I noticed that he was shirtless and wearing just a pair of shorts.

"Get in here." He caught my hand and tugged me into his room.

Within a split-second I was alone in the dark with a nearly naked boy whose name I wasn't even sure I really knew. Was Nico a nickname?

I backed up against the door as he whipped the baseball cap off the top of my head and set my hair free.

"I just wanted to make sure you were okay."

"You did, huh?" He shook his head. "Did you really think this disguise would work?"

"I'm here, aren't I?" I crossed my arms.

"Yes, you are." He set the baseball cap on his head backwards and studied me. "I'm sorry about last night."

"Are you?" I held up my phone. "Because I didn't hear a

word from you. Did you think I wouldn't wonder what happened to you?"

"I thought you wouldn't want to have anything to do with me after what happened."

"I don't." I cleared my throat. "I mean, I just wanted to make sure you weren't locked up somewhere."

"They haven't made a cage that can hold me." He smirked.

"Is that supposed to be funny?"

He sighed as he turned away from me.

I watched the muscles in his back tense as his arms stretched and then crossed over his chest.

He turned back to face me, the smirk gone. His eyes hardened as they settled on me.

"Things weren't supposed to happen that way."

"So tell me the truth." I started toward him. "Just tell me what's going on, Nicholas."

"No." He took a step back. "No, it's better if I don't."

"Seriously? Do you expect me to be satisfied with that?"

"No." He licked his lips, then took a breath. "But you're going to have to be."

"No." I pursed my lips.

"Man." He looked at me intently, his eyes wide and his lips parted. "How am I supposed to resist you when you look at me like that?"

"Resist me?" I glared at him. "Is that your plan? To try to turn this into some kind of hook-up?"

"You're the one who broke into the boys' dorm and woke me up." He shifted closer to me, his eyes still locked to mine. "Were you up all night thinking about me?"

"I was up all night thinking about whether I could have done something to help you." I glared at him as he reached for my hand. "But clearly, the same concerns didn't keep you up."

"I got back an hour ago." He traced his fingertips across the curve of my wrist but he didn't take my hand. "You have no idea what I was thinking about."

"Then tell me." I searched his eyes for the boy I'd shared the universe with hours before.

He clenched his jaw, curled his fingers around mine, and pulled me close to him in a sudden and forceful motion.

I gasped and looked into his eyes as he spoke.

"I was thinking that I'd just lost the best thing that has ever happened to me and I would do anything to get her back."

My heart raced as I felt his bare chest brush against my arm and noticed his full lips drawing close to mine. I could have kissed him right then and he wouldn't have stopped me. I could have kissed him and probably done a lot more. The moment was thick with the promise of exploring the intense connection between us. My body pulsated with demands that I couldn't even identify.

Dizzy with passion and confusion, I stared at him. "I guess that's what you say to all the girls, right?"

FIFTEEN

His eyes narrowed. He released my hand, then shook his head. "Why did you really come here?"

"I told you why." I took a step back from him—just so that I could breathe—as my head swam.

"You just wanted to check on the con artist, on the guy whose only goal is to scam you?"

"Am I supposed to see you as anything else?" My chest tightened. I knew I saw him as something else. But he didn't need to know that. "You won't tell me anything about yourself. You're always trying to be cool, detached, smug."

"Ouch." He tipped his head to the side and rolled his eyes. "Anything else to say?"

"Ugh! You are so frustrating." I glared at him. "I just hate it!"

"Hate me?" He settled his hand on the curve of my hip and looked into my eyes.

"I hate this!" I shoved his hand away. "I hate feeling like you're just trying to get something from me—that I'll just be another girl on your list."

He tightened his lips as he studied me, but he didn't say a word.

In the quiet, I heard my own voice echoing back through my thoughts. Loud and ragged, as if I was out of breath.

Embarrassed and infuriated, I turned toward the door. "Never mind. I never should have come here." I reached for the doorknob.

Before I could grab it, his hand caught my wrist. He spun me back toward him.

"Stop!" I yanked my hand away. "I'm not them, do you understand me? I'm not going to be them! It's just not who I am! I don't want to fall for someone, get conned into believing they feel the same way and then have them walk away from me like I'm nothing!"

"Your hat." He whispered as he held it out to me. "You forgot your hat."

I snatched it from his hand as my cheeks throbbed with heat. I piled my hair on top of my head and shoved the hat down. My hands shook from the emotions that pulsated through me.

"Here." He tucked some loose hair under the edge of the hat. His fingertips caressed my cheek as his hand fell away. "You shouldn't, you know."

"I shouldn't what?" I fought the urge to curse at him—or to kiss him. Both desires seemed to surge through me.

"Fall for me." He placed his hands against the door on either side of me. His arms just barely grazed my shoulders.

"I know." I bit into my bottom lip and tried not to breathe in the scent of him.

"You're right. I'm not the right person for you." He looked into my eyes. "You deserve someone who tells the truth. Someone who doesn't have secrets. Someone who doesn't get you carted off in a police car."

"I do." My heart pounded.

"You do." He closed his eyes and touched his forehead to mine. "I hope you find that person." He took a sharp breath. "But you could never, ever, be nothing to me." He drew his head back and looked into my eyes again. "You don't have to believe a word I say. But that will always be true." He dropped his hands from the door and took a step back. "You should go. Everyone will be getting up soon."

I didn't want to go. I'd never wanted to stay in one place so much in my life. I wanted to throw my arms around him and promise him that I didn't care about his secrets or his lies. I wanted to tell him that he didn't have to pretend anymore, that he could just relax with me.

But my hand curled around the doorknob behind me.

Soon the boys' dormitory would be alive with all of my male classmates. They would see me leave Nicholas's room first thing in the morning. They would suspect why I'd been there and what it meant. I'd never be able to live it down.

And if I stayed?

He put his hand over mine and turned the knob on the door for me, then pulled it open a few inches.

"Go."

"I came here to make sure that you're okay." I stumbled over my words as I pulled open the door a few more inches.

"I'm okay." He smiled, then shrugged. "Cool, detached, and smug, right?" He smirked.

I turned and stepped out the door. As I hurried down the hallway to the stairs, I fought the desire to turn back. I heard his door click shut. He'd told me to leave. He'd told me that I shouldn't fall for him.

I reached the bottom step and felt my heart drop. It was already too late. I knew that now. I shouldn't have, but I had.

I glanced back up the stairs just in time to see Wes at the top of them.

He stared down at me, then looked in the direction of Nicholas's room. When he looked back at me, I could see the frustration in his expression.

I didn't stick around a second longer. I brushed quickly past the guard and out into the common room. Then I raced up the stairs to the girls' dormitory.

"Wait just a second!" One of the dorm monitors caught me by the arm. "This is the girls' dorm."

I pulled off my hat and my hair tumbled down against my cheeks and neck. I remembered the way his fingertips felt as they'd caressed my cheek. I remembered the closeness of his forehead against mine and his whispered promise.

"Sorry, my mistake." The monitor laughed, then continued on down the stairs.

I headed for my dorm room, flung the door open, and tossed myself down on the sofa.

How was I supposed to survive his saying that to me? How was I supposed to move on when it felt impossible to think of anyone but him?

"Well, well, well." Apple dropped onto the sofa as well— right on top of my feet—and looked over at me.

"Go away." I covered my face with a pillow.

"Oh, sorry. It's my job to inform you of the intervention."

"The what?" I moved the pillow and pulled my feet out from under her.

"Be at the hideout at lunch." She looked me straight in the eyes. "Or we'll hunt you down."

"Okay?" I frowned. "Why?"

"Just be there." She gave my feet a light slap. "And seriously, skip a few classes today, you look exhausted."

"I am pretty tired." I closed my eyes and covered my face with the pillow again.

Why not skip a few classes? I'd already broken more rules than I ever had before. I'd already practically been arrested.

Apple went to the kitchen to make her breakfast and I sprawled out on the sofa. My body ached with exhaustion, but my mind still spun with everything that Nicholas had said to me.

What secrets could he be keeping? Could I really believe what he said?

I recalled what the police officer had said about me being the only girl that had actually gone up on the platform with Nicholas. That meant that Nicholas had been telling me the truth. Which meant two things.

I was a fool for going up there in the first place and maybe, just maybe, Nicholas really did have genuine feelings for me. But did that really matter? Clearly, he wasn't going to change for me. He'd told me to my face that I shouldn't fall for him, that I deserved better.

But what if I didn't want anyone but him?

As I began to drift off to sleep, I thought about how it had felt to look up at the sky with his arm around me. That was exactly where I wanted to be—caught in the swirl of what stars we could see and the lights of the city—with everything else left far below us.

That moment was Nicholas, and that was the Nicholas that I wasn't sure I could live without.

SIXTEEN

By the time I woke up, a few hours had passed. My mind swam as I tried to pick apart my memories from my dreams. Had all of it really happened?

Groggy and confused I stood up from the sofa. I recalled his forehead pressed against mine. My heart skipped a beat.

Yes, there it was, the certainty that I'd flipped completely head over heels over a boy I barely knew. Was that really possible when I'd only spent one evening out with him? One amazing evening. One evening that I knew I would never get with anyone else.

My phone buzzed with a text. I snatched it up, eager to see a message from Nicholas.

Instead, it was from Apple.

AT THE HIDEOUT. Where are you?

I WINCED as I realized it was already lunchtime. After a quick splash of water on my face, I hurried out of my dorm room, down the steps, through the common room, and out into the courtyard. A few students sat on the benches there eating their lunches, but most were in the cafeteria or the library.

Normally, I would hide out in the library and try to sort out my feelings about everything. Instead, I marched toward the hideout. I didn't know exactly what my friends had planned, but I guessed that it wasn't going to be pleasant.

The closer I came to the building, the more annoyed I felt. I loved that I had such a close group of friends around me, but why should they get any say in my life choices?

"I'm here." I pushed through the door and walked right into the middle of a semi-circle of friends.

"It's about time." Wes frowned.

"Ease up." Maby shot him a warning look.

"Ease up?" He shook his head. "Not after what I saw this morning."

"I should have known." I crossed my arms as I stared at the group gathered around me. "This is about Nicholas?"

"Of course." Wes looked over at Fifi. "She was in his room all night."

"I was not." My cheeks warmed. "I was not in there all night, not that it would be any of your business if I was."

"How is it not my business?" Wes scowled. "I care about you and I warned you not to get involved with him."

"But you wouldn't tell me why!" I threw my hands up in the air. "How am I supposed to know to stay away, if you won't tell me why I should stay away?"

"You could try just trusting me." He shrugged.

"Why not tell her?" Maby looked over at Wes. "You're the one who brought us all together here—because you said it was so urgent. So tell her, and all of us, what is so terrible about her being with Nicholas?" She glanced over at me. "Not that I agree with it, but she is free to make her own choices."

"Thanks. I think." I quirked an eyebrow.

"I can't tell you because I promised not to. In fact, I could even get in legal trouble if I do tell you." Wes shoved his hands into his pockets. "That's why I'm asking you to trust me."

"I can't do that." I shook my head. "I can't deal with any more lies or secrets. He won't tell me, you won't tell me, but everyone thinks that they get to decide what I'm going to do with my life. Why don't I have a say in any of this?"

"You do." Apple took my hand. "Of course you do. We just don't want to see you get hurt."

"Maybe I want to get hurt." I took a sharp breath as I heard my own words. "Maybe I want to feel something, anything at all. Maybe it would be worse to never know what all this craziness going on inside of me is about than it would be to be hurt."

"Candy, just think about this." Maby took a step closer to me. "His reputation is really not good. All I hear are stories about him serial dating, and even then, he's not exactly a gentleman about it."

"So?" I shrugged. "So what? Maybe I want to be a fool for once. Maybe I just want to know what it's like to have someone look at me the way he does, even if it's a lie."

"Someone will." Apple squeezed my hand. "Someone better than him."

Her words echoed through my mind. Isn't that what Nicholas had said to me? That I deserved better? But I didn't want better.

"You know what? Thank you." I looked around at each of my friends. I took a step back toward the door. "I know that this was planned out of love. I know that you are all looking out for me. And honestly, I feel so lucky to have such good friends like you." I took a deep breath. "But this just made me realize what I really want. So, if you'll excuse me, I have something important to do."

"What?" Wes tried to meet my eyes.

"I have a choice to make." I turned and stepped out of the building. I had no idea where Nicholas might be, but I knew that I had to see him as soon as possible.

I pulled out my phone and typed out a text to him.

MEET ME IN THE COURTYARD. *I need to talk to you. I'll be waiting.*

I WALKED over to one of the benches in the courtyard and sat down. As I watched the other students stroll back and forth, heading for their next class, I felt no pang of guilt. I'd never skipped classes before. Today, I needed to handle something more important than textbooks.

As the courtyard emptied, I glanced at my phone.

No response. Had he even read the text? I stood up and began to pace back and forth. Maybe he was stuck in a class-room. Maybe he couldn't get away from whatever he was doing. Maybe he hadn't even looked at his phone.

I sat back down and tried to be patient. Now that I knew what I wanted, I couldn't wait to tell him. I couldn't wait to see the look in his eyes when I made my choice.

Minutes passed. Several of them. I checked my phone again.

Still no response.

Maybe it hadn't gone through? Sometimes my service could act a little funny. I typed out another text.

· · ·

I'M IN THE COURTYARD. I need to talk to you.

AS I STARED at the phone, I willed him to text me back. Even if it was just some silly symbol or a single letter. Anything to let me know that he'd at least gotten the text.

But minutes continued to pass by without any kind of response. My heart sank as the courtyard filled with students again, each hurrying to their next class.

Maybe he just didn't want to see me. Maybe he'd realized his mistake and he didn't want to encourage my desperation.

Embarrassed, I stood up from the bench and watched the crowd pass by. As it began to thin out, I wondered if I'd completely lost my mind.

Suddenly I felt a hand on my wrist. It wrapped around it and tugged until I was pulled back behind one of the tall wide statues in the far side of the courtyard.

"Nicholas?" I looked into his eyes as he turned me to face him.

"You can't do that."

"Can't do what?" I frowned.

"Sit there out in the open and expect me to come to you." He brushed my hair back over my shoulders. "What's going on? Why did you want to see me?"

"What's so wrong with being seen with me?"

"I asked you first." He guided me back against the statue and left only a few inches of space between us. "So, what do you need to talk to me about? I thought I'd made things pretty clear this morning."

"You did." I stared straight into his eyes. "But it's not just your choice to make."

"It isn't?" He smiled some.

"No."

"And?" He leaned forward enough that a few of his curls tickled against the strands of hair that had drifted forward into my face again.

"And I don't care if I get hurt. I don't care about your secrets or your lies."

SEVENTEEN

"Candace." He sighed as he stared intently at me. "It's not as easy as that."

"Why not?" I searched his eyes as my heart pounded. "It can be easy. It can be whatever we let it be."

"I wish it could be." He frowned.

"It can be. Unless you don't want it to be." I leaned back against the statue and lowered my eyes. "I'm such an idiot."

"You're not." His fingers laced through mine. "It's just that things are a little more complicated than you think."

"I don't care how complicated they are." I looked back into his eyes. "I'm not asking for anything but a chance. I don't need to be your girlfriend. I don't need to know every detail of your life. I just don't want this to be the last time we're together."

"Being seen with me will only ruin your reputation." He took a step back and shook his head. "It just isn't fair to you. Can't you see that?"

"Can I see that everyone around me seems to think it's their job to make decisions for me?" I raised an eyebrow. "Yes, that is becoming very clear to me."

"It's not about that." He narrowed his eyes. "You don't know the whole situation. I do. I have to make the right decision to make sure you're not hurt in all this."

"But you have no problem doing the same thing with any other girl?" I shook my head. "Don't think I haven't heard the stories. You told me yourself that you do this kind of thing all the time. If this isn't what you want, then just tell me. Don't make it seem like it's about more than what it is."

"Stop saying that." He took both of my hands and held them firmly with his own. "I wouldn't be doing the same thing with you. That's the part that you don't get. Those other girls— they're not you. I didn't even know girls like you existed until I saw you one day. You were standing up for your friend. This quiet girl who I'd barely noticed had turned into this lioness ready to pounce. I'd never seen such fierceness in anyone before. And then, just like that, you turned right back into this quiet girl. Only I couldn't stop noticing you after that. I never should have tried to start something with you. I had no idea what I was getting us both into. That's my fault. I'm sorry." He ran his thumbs along the backs of my hands. "It was selfish of me." He whispered. "I just couldn't resist."

"You don't have to resist, I'm right here." I held his gaze. "I'm right here in front of you and I'm not afraid."

"You should be."

"I'm not."

"You will be." He sighed as he released my hands again. "I can't, I just can't do this."

"Then you're the coward." I took the chance to slip away from him as anger rushed through me. I'd never pleaded with a boy to like me, to kiss me, to give me a chance. I'd made myself ultimately vulnerable by admitting my feelings for him and my willingness to take a chance. But that wasn't enough for him. "You're right, maybe I do have the wrong idea about you." I started back toward the dormitories, then paused after a few steps. I turned back and spotted him with his forearm resting against the statue and his head against the sleeve of his shirt. "You're not going to come after me?"

"I shouldn't." He refused to look at me.

"Great." I shrugged. "I guess I'll just take that as a clear statement of how you feel about me."

"You know better than that." He lifted his head. "You know exactly how I feel about you."

"No, I don't." I held out my hands. "I don't have a clue. Because if you were telling me the truth about how you felt about me, you wouldn't let me walk away from you."

"I'm letting you walk away because it's the right thing to do." He walked toward me.

"And when have you ever done the right thing?" I pursed my lips.

"Unbelievable." He groaned as he suddenly wrapped his arms around me and swept my body close to his. "You are unbelievable."

A rush of pleasure took my breath away as he held me tight. I wanted to stay in that moment for as long as I possibly could. As I stared into his eyes, I could read the fear and uncertainty beneath the confidence that usually inhabited them.

"I won't hurt you," I whispered as his lips brushed along the curve of my cheek, then buried themselves in my hair along the side of my neck.

I trailed my fingertips down the length of his back and felt him shiver.

"Candace, we really shouldn't." His arms tightened even more.

"I've lost so many people in my life, Nicholas." My heart fluttered as I wondered if confessing that might make him even more hesitant. "I've lost both of my parents and more friends than I can count. I can't explain the way I feel about you. But I do know that I don't want to lose you." I looked into his eyes. "Is that such a terrible thing?"

"No." He trailed his fingers back through my hair. "No, it's not terrible at all. I don't think anyone has ever wanted me around—not really—not unless it was because I could do something for them." He searched my eyes. "But I don't want to be another person that hurts you. Can't you understand that?"

"What you don't understand is that if you give up on this, on whatever might be between us, that's what will hurt me." I pulled away from his embrace and frowned. "It's too late. You showed me the universe and now I'm lost in it." I glanced up at him. "Lost in you."

He clenched his jaw, then looked up at the sky before he looked back at me. As he took a slow breath, I prepared myself for his rejection. He had every reason not to want me. He had every reason to tell me to walk away or to walk away himself.

"No one can know." He exhaled as he settled his gaze on me. "Alright?"

"Alright." My heart raced. Was that a yes?

"I mean no one." He narrowed his eyes. "You have to sell it hard. Because if someone finds out, it's going to mean trouble for both of us."

"Okay." I nodded as a smile tugged at my lips. "I can keep a secret. Trust me."

"I am." He cupped my cheeks with his warm palms and stared straight into my eyes. "And you have to trust me too when I say that we need to give it some time. Get to know each other. Things are different between us. I want to know why. I want to know everything about you. Can we do that? Can we start off as friends and see where things take us?"

My heart sank. There it was—the "friend" word. But I couldn't disagree with him. I didn't really know anything about him. I knew he had secrets that he wouldn't reveal to me, but what about his likes and dislikes? What about his musical tastes? What did he want from life? What had he already experienced? Going slow did make the most sense.

"Yes." I placed my hands over his and smiled. "We can do that."

"Good." He smiled and let his hands slide back to my shoulders.

As he pulled me in for another hug, it took all my strength to resist attempting a kiss. Slow, I reminded myself. I didn't know why we had to hide or what terrible things could happen if anyone found out, but I did know that I wanted him to be part of my life.

I'd follow his rules—whatever they were—if it meant I had the chance to discover more about him.

EIGHTEEN

"Go." He tipped his head toward the dormitories as another rush of students emptied out of the classrooms and into the courtyard.

I took a step back from him and held my breath as the crowd swept him away from me. I'd promised him that I could keep it a secret, but my heart threatened to burst with excitement.

What could be better than a secret love affair? I'd never imagined I could stumble into my own love story, but here I was. No, it wasn't perfect and I couldn't be sure if it really qualified as a love story just yet, but it was something. It was far more than I'd ever experienced before.

As I headed back toward the girls' dormitories, my friend Jenny caught me by the arm.

"I've been looking for you! I couldn't believe you took off out of the hideout like that." She frowned as she looked into my eyes. "Are you okay?"

"Fine." I nodded.

"Are you sure? You seemed so upset when you left. You know that we are all just looking out for you, right?"

"I know." I took a deep breath. "And you were all right."

"We were?"

"Yes. He's exactly what everyone warned me about. I thought maybe there could be something more between us, but I guess I'd lost my mind." I shrugged. "I'm as alone as ever."

"Aw, Candy." She hugged me. "Don't look at it that way. You avoided a heartbreak. That's a good thing."

"Sure. You're right." I hugged her in return. "I think I'm just going to lay low for the rest of the day. I claimed a sick day, so I'd better not let any of the teachers catch me roaming around."

"True." She glanced past me at the group of students that was headed for one of the classrooms. "I've got to hurry or I'm going to be late to class. Are you sure you're okay?"

"I'm fine." I smiled again.

"Find me later, okay? There's something I want to talk to you about."

"Okay." I caught her arm as she started to walk away. "Is everything okay with you?"

"Great." She nodded. "I have some great news to share with you. I told everyone else after you left. But I have to go right now." She broke into a jog toward her classroom.

I recalled how frustrated I'd been with my circle of friends earlier in the day. As I walked toward the dormitories, I reminded myself yet again that I was lucky to have so many people that cared so much about me. But that only made my stomach churn.

I didn't like the idea of lying to them all. But what choice did I have? I'd promised to keep my relationship with Nicholas a secret and I was determined to do just that.

My first test came when Apple returned to our dorm room after completing her classes for the day.

"Hi, you." She smiled as she sat down beside me on the sofa. "Are you still talking to me?"

"Of course I am." I nudged her with my elbow. "Why wouldn't I be?"

"I know that you probably thought the intervention was a little over the top." She winced. "Even I did, honestly."

"I'm sure it was mostly Wes's idea." I rolled my eyes. "And I'm also sure that his heart was in the right place." I sighed. "But no one has to worry about it anymore. He was right. All of you were right. Nicholas isn't the right person for me and he made that clear today. So, I guess I lost my mind for a few minutes. Maybe I just wanted to find someone to share things with."

"Speaking of that." Apple grinned. "You have to come to dinner tonight. Promise?"

"Sure." I patted my stomach. "I'm starving actually. Why?"

"There's this guy." She wiggled on the sofa and grinned.

"Guy?" My heart skipped a beat.

"Yes. He's a friend of mine. He is a year younger than you, but he's fantastic. He's an artist and he loves to make things with sea glass and things like that." She held out her wrist. "He made this bracelet."

"Pretty." I nodded. "But I'm not really interested in meeting anyone right now."

"Oh, but you have to be. It will be the perfect way to get your mind off of Nicholas and get Wes off your back." She patted the back of my hand. "You don't have to do anything but show up tonight and see what you think. That's all I'm asking."

I rolled the idea around in my mind for a moment. I had zero interest in anyone other than Nicholas, but she couldn't know that. Maybe she was right. Maybe showing interest in another guy would be the perfect cover to make sure that no one suspected Nicholas and I had something of our own going on in secret.

Something. I closed my eyes. I had no idea what that something even was anymore.

"Sure, I'll be there." I smiled at Apple. "Thanks for thinking of me. You're a great friend."

"I'm trying to be. I know we've all been neglecting you a bit lately—caught up in our own things—and I'm sorry about that."

"No need to apologize, I'm happy for all of you." I stood up from the sofa. "I'm not going to make it to dinner without a snack. Do you want anything?"

"No, thanks, I'm going to grab a pretzel on my way to meet..." She stopped talking, then sighed. "There I go again, neglecting you."

"Would you stop?" I laughed. "Go and have your fun. I'm just going to eat something, then grab a quick nap. I'm still pretty tired."

"Are you sure? Because I can blow him off. I can stay right here with you." She looked into my eyes.

"I'm sure, Apple. Now go and have your fun." I shooed her toward the door. "I could use the quiet, to be honest."

"Alright, but if you get bored and you want me to come back, I'm only a text away."

"Great, thanks." I smiled as she walked out the door.

Only a text away. Would Nicholas answer me if I texted him? I wasn't sure what exactly the rules were in our secret friendship.

I popped some popcorn then stretched out on the sofa. As I munched on my snack, I composed what I hoped would be the perfect text. Not too clingy, not too desperate—just a text that let him know I was available to talk.

THANKS FOR THIS AFTERNOON. I'm glad we made things clear. Let me know if you're ever free to talk.

. . .

I BIT into my bottom lip as I read it over. Maybe it wasn't perfect. Maybe what we had wasn't perfect either. But I was really curious about where it might lead.

Moments later I received a text in return.

CAN'T STOP THINKING *about you. Can we meet tonight? You know where. I promise no cops this time.*

I SMILED AT THE THOUGHT. My heart pounded. Hours stood between me and seeing Nicholas again—long tormenting hours. But just knowing we had plans to get together made the time bearable. It sure seemed like he wanted to see me just as much.

I closed my eyes and imagined what it would have been like to kiss him up on that platform, under what stars we could see, with the flashing lights of the police car beneath us.

Maybe one day I'd have the chance to find out.

NINETEEN

By the time I headed to the cafeteria, my mind buzzed with excitement—not to meet the guy that Apple wanted to introduce me to, but to sneak out later in the evening and meet Nicholas. I already had a list of questions in my head to ask him. Questions that I thought would be safe and not conflict with his need to keep secrets.

I strolled into the cafeteria and headed straight for the food line. The popcorn had done nothing to quell my hunger. I wasn't sure that I'd ever felt so hungry in my life. Maybe it was all the excitement or maybe it was the way I'd been completely losing track of time and missing meals. Either way, the entire cafeteria smelled delicious to me.

Once I had my tray, I walked over to our lunch table already filled with my friends and sat down across from Jenny.

"What are you smiling about?" Jenny scrunched up her nose. "It's meatloaf night."

"I don't care what it is, I'm starving." I laughed as I picked up my fork.

"Listen, Candy, about earlier." Wes cleared his throat.

"Don't worry about it. You were right, he's a jerk. Let's

move on, okay?" I flashed him a smile, then took a bite of my meatloaf. It didn't taste as good as I'd hoped, but it was still food.

"Oh, there he is!" Apple stood up and waved to someone who had just walked into the cafeteria.

I turned to look and saw a young man with a handsome sweet face and another person who stepped in behind him. My heart pounded as my eyes met Nicholas's.

He stared at me.

I quickly looked away and turned back to the others at the table. I had to play the role, even if that meant being deafened by the pounding of my heartbeat.

"So? What do you think?" Apple whispered to me as the other boy began walking toward the table. "His name is Ethan."

"He's cute." I smiled.

"Hi." Ethan stepped up beside me and eyed the empty seat next to me.

"Hi. I'm Candace." I gestured to the seat. "Please, join us."

"Great." He nodded as he sat down and gave a nervous laugh. "Thanks for the invitation, Apple."

So polite. I forced a smile. Nothing cool or detached about this one. His short blond hair was carefully combed and his uniform was spotless.

"I was telling Ethan about your work supporting the rain forest and he got so excited. Didn't you, Ethan?" Apple met his eyes.

"I don't know if excited is the right word." He shrugged. "It's just that I recently had a chance to travel through some of the rain forest and it was spectacular. I have some pictures if you'd like to see." He held his phone out to me.

"Sure." I took his phone and began to flip through the pictures. "Oh wow, these are really great." I lost myself in the beauty of the snapshots. "It must have been such an amazing experience for you. Is this your family?" I smiled as I looked at the photograph of him with three other people.

"Uh—yes, those are my parents—and my girlfriend." He coughed. "I mean, ex-girlfriend."

"I'm sorry." I met his eyes. "I just made things awkward, didn't I?"

"It's okay." He smiled. "It was an amazing experience. My dad gets to travel a lot with his work, so we've been a few times. We try to go once every year or so to keep up with what's going on."

"That's a great thing to do. I'd love to go sometime. Maybe over the summer." I handed him back his phone. "Thanks for sharing these with me."

"Sure." He began to talk about his visit and soon I was enthralled with stories about the different animals he'd seen and what the locals were like. I did find myself hanging on his every word as I tried to imagine being right there with him.

Soon my friends had finished their dinner and one by one they began to leave the table. But Ethan and I continued to chat.

"Would you like to take a walk with me?" He stood up and picked up both of our empty trays. "It's a nice evening."

"That would be great." I glanced at the time on my phone. "It'll have to be a short one though. Sorry, I have somewhere I need to be."

"Oh?" He met my eyes as he set the trays on a nearby cart. "What are you up to?"

I thought about how to answer him. What was I up to? I wanted to sneak off and see an amazing person that I couldn't wait to spend time with. But Ethan was interesting to talk to and I loved hearing about his travels. I could easily see us becoming good friends.

"It's just a project I'm working on. It's due by the end of the week and I'm a little behind."

"I could help you." He smiled. "I mean, if you'd like that."

"Oh, thanks." I forced a smile as my heart raced. I'd never been very good at lying. "But it's really a solo thing. I wouldn't want to break any rules."

"Oh, I don't blame you. I think honesty is so important." He held the door of the cafeteria open for me as I stepped outside. "Don't you?"

"Yes." I bit into my bottom lip.

"I really admire you for wanting to make sure you do the project yourself. Most people will do anything to get a good grade, especially around here." He settled into a mild stroll.

"There's so much pressure." I matched his pace.

"Yes, but that's no excuse." His hand brushed against mine. "If people would just be straightforward—not keep secrets, not lie all the time—the world would be a much better place, don't you think?"

"In most cases, yes." I edged a little bit further away from him to avoid his touch.

"See, I don't think there are any exceptions." He shook his head. "That's the problem. We have morals and then we bend them, because we think that right and wrong can be blurry. But they can't. It's like my ex-girlfriend—she lied to me about a few things. I found out. Then she lied some more."

"Oh no, was she cheating on you?" I frowned.

"No, nothing like that, but she didn't tell the truth about some of the things that happened to her in the past and when I called her out on it she acted like it was no big deal." He narrowed his eyes. "I just can't tolerate that."

"I see." I paused as we reached the courtyard.

"Do you want to sit?" He gestured to one of the benches.

"Sure." I glanced at my phone again to check the time. I smiled as I counted down the minutes in my head.

He sat down beside me, very close to me. "So, Apple told

me that you might be open to meeting someone new."

"Did she?" I stared down at my shoes.

"I'm someone new." He rested his hand on top of mine on the bench.

I knew that if I jerked my hand back, I would send the signal that I wasn't interested. But wouldn't his presence be the perfect cover?

I looked into his eyes and smiled. "I'm sorry, I'm just a little nervous."

"Why?" He squeezed my hand. "I don't bite. I promise."

"That's good." I laughed.

"Unless you want me to." He offered a pretend growl.

I did my best not to roll my eyes. "Easy there, tiger."

"Tiger, I like that. Maybe that'll be your nickname for me."

"Maybe." I shrugged.

Suddenly he leaned toward me, his lips puckered and headed straight for mine.

I took a sharp breath and turned my head just in time for his lips to land on my cheek.

"Too soon?" He winced as he leaned back. "I'm sorry. It's just that I heard you might have been interested in Nicholas Holden, so I thought maybe you liked the guy to make the first move."

"You heard wrong." I frowned. "There is nothing between Nicholas and me."

"Sorry, that was stupid." He groaned.

"Don't worry about it." I squeezed his hand. "I'd just like to take things slow, if that's okay."

"Sure." He smiled as he met my eyes. "We can do that."

As we walked toward the dormitories, I felt a strange sensation in the pit of my stomach. Was it wrong to let Ethan think he had a chance with me when I couldn't wait to sneak off and meet Nicholas?

TWENTY

The minutes couldn't slip by fast enough. I tried to distract myself by watching a movie with Apple, but my thoughts kept turning right back to Nicholas.

"So?" Apple tossed some popcorn into her mouth.

"So?" I looked over at her.

"So what did you think of him?"

"Who?"

"Who?" Apple laughed. "The boy you almost kissed tonight."

"Oh, right." I smiled. "He seems nice."

"Nice? Ugh, that's the kiss of death." She flopped her head back against my shoulder and looked into my eyes. "Not interested?"

"It's not the kiss of death." I frowned. "Considering the close brush I'd had with someone who is not in any way nice, nice is a huge compliment." I shrugged. "He's cute too. The kiss? That was a little surprising."

"I noticed. He's usually pretty shy. He must really like you."

Guilt rippled through me. I did my best to ignore it. "I'm looking forward to seeing him again." I glanced at my phone. "I guess I'd better get to work on that project. I'll probably be in the library really late tonight, so don't wait up."

"Alright, but don't get yourself into any more trouble. You're starting to get a reputation for being wild, and you know I can't hang around with people like that."

"Ha ha." I snatched some popcorn from her bowl and tossed it at her.

"Hey! Don't start a war you don't intend to finish." She picked up the bowl and threatened to toss the rest of the popcorn at me.

"Okay, okay, I surrender!" I laughed as I headed for the door.

As soon as I was in the courtyard my heart started to pound. What if he wasn't there? What if he was?

The thought of being close to him again thrilled me. But I knew that I needed to restrain myself. Whatever happened between us had to remain a secret and that meant that I needed to make sure that what happened between us wasn't so wonderful that I had to tell someone about it.

As I slipped through the gap in the fence, I thought about the fact that just a short time ago I would never have considered sneaking off campus. What was it about Nicholas that made me take so many wild chances? I had no idea, but the thrill I felt as I ran down the sidewalk made me certain that I wanted to find out.

I met my cab driver at the corner and settled into the back seat. I pulled out my phone and checked for any new texts.

"Nothing." I frowned as I scrolled through to make sure.

He'd asked me to meet him. He didn't say that he would text me, but a little reassurance would have gone a long way. He'd told me I'd know where to meet him. The only place I could think of was on the bridge. But what if that wasn't what he meant?

"Are you sure you want me to let you off here?" The cab driver glanced back at me. "It's not exactly the safest place."

"I'll be fine, thanks." I paid him the fare, then stepped out of the car.

"Are you meeting someone?" He frowned. "I can wait a bit if you need me to."

"No, I'll be fine, thanks."

As soon as the cab drove away, I questioned my sanity. There I was, surrounded by strangers on the Brooklyn Bridge. I studied each face that passed me, but none belonged to Nicholas.

As the minutes slipped by, I wondered if he might have forgotten. Or maybe this was his way of making it clear to me that we didn't belong together—that I needed to back off.

An ache formed in the pit of my stomach as I thought about calling the cab driver back. I wanted the night to be magical, but it now had the potential of turning into a nightmare.

I took a step back and looked up at the platform that we had spent time on together. Maybe that was where he wanted me to be? There was no sign of him there either. I didn't have any interest in being caught by the police again.

I sighed as I leaned back against the railing and watched the cars pass by. Maybe I had let myself get lost in the idea that Nicholas had feelings for me. Was I just stalking him at this point? Desperate for his attention?

I closed my eyes and heard my grandmother's voice in my mind.

"Always stand proud, no matter the circumstance. You have the right to be exactly who you right now."

Who I was right now was a heartbroken teenager, lovesick and pathetic, lost in a crowd of people who wouldn't notice if I disappeared. With my hands shoved in my pockets, I turned to walk to the end of the bridge.

Just as I took my first step, I spotted him.

A few steps away, half-hidden by his hoodie and gazing at the water beyond the railing, I could have easily overlooked him. Instead, my heart stopped and my body froze. He tilted his head just enough to look at me.

The moment our eyes met, my heart beat again, then raced. I started to move toward him.

He looked back down at the water. I noticed his hands curled around the railing, so tight that his knuckles blanched white.

"I didn't think you would come." He murmured his words as I stepped up beside him.

"You didn't think I would come?" I leaned against the railing beside him. "I'm the one that has been waiting for you."

"I've been here." He licked his lips as he stared hard at the water. "I just didn't know what to say."

"Remember, we don't have to worry about any of that." I placed my hand over his on the railing and smiled. "This is just us, right? No need to hide."

"Just us?" He yanked his hand away from my touch and created some space between us as he turned to face me. "Don't you mean just us and that boy in the cafeteria?"

I stared at him, at the pain etched into the tense muscles of his face. I heard the tremor in his voice and suddenly I understood why he'd stood there watching me for so long.

"You saw that?"

"Yes, I saw that." He turned back to the railing. "How could I not?"

"It's not what you think."

"It sure looked like it." He looked back at me. "He kissed you."

"He tried."

"He kissed you." He stepped closer to me, his eyes locked to mine. "Don't tell me I didn't see what I saw."

"Nicholas." I shifted back away from him until I felt my back against the railing of the bridge. "He tried to kiss me. I turned my head."

"And?"

"And what?" My chest grew tight as I held my breath.

"And what did you say to him when he tried to kiss you? Did you tell him to get lost? Did you push him away?" He continued to hold my gaze. "Because from what I saw, you didn't do any of those things."

"No." I forced myself to take a deep breath. "I didn't do any of those things. I smiled at him."

"You smiled at him." He looked up at the sky, then back at me. "But you came here tonight to be with me?"

"Of course I did." I slid my arm around his waist. "I smiled at him—for you."

"That doesn't make sense." He frowned as he studied me. "Are you trying to make me jealous? Is that it? So that I'll lose my mind?"

"Are you jealous?" I raised an eyebrow. "I didn't expect that."

"Why not?"

"Because it's not like you don't play the field."

"I told you." He rested his hands on my shoulders and looked straight into my eyes. "It's different with you. I thought it was different for you too."

TWENTY-ONE

"It is."

"Don't say it if you don't mean it." He started to step around me.

"Stop." I placed my hand on his chest and felt the hammering of his heartbeat as he looked back at me. "Nicholas, you wanted all this to be a secret. I thought, what better way to throw everyone off than for me to play along a little with Ethan? I mean, no one is going to suspect we're together if I'm spending time with Ethan."

"Seriously?" He sighed as he studied me.

"I thought it was a good idea." I frowned.

"It was." He shook his head. "I just wish I'd been in on it."

"I didn't mean to make you jealous." I bit into my bottom lip. "Honestly, I didn't think you would be."

"I was." He shoved his hands into his pockets. "It's a new experience for me too. I'm sorry for overreacting. It's just that when I saw him with you, I realized I couldn't stand the thought of losing you." He lowered his voice as he leaned closer to me. "I've never felt like this about anyone before. But we have to be careful." He winced. "I don't know if this is such a good idea."

"It's just us, remember?" I took his hand and looked into his eyes. "This is our time. No one else has to know."

"Just us." He nodded, then tugged me forward. "I want to take you somewhere."

"Am I going to have to climb?" I smiled.

"Not this time." He tugged me forward and across the bridge.

As I chased after him, I felt that rush again. Not because I might get in trouble or because the wind blew through my hair or because it felt as if we'd slipped into another universe, but because when he looked over his shoulder at me, nothing else mattered. All reason, all logic that had steered me in the right direction in the past, vanished beneath my desire to see his smile. It was a pure and unexpected feeling that I had no way to define. But it was more powerful than anything I'd ever experienced before.

When he finally stopped, it was at the entrance of a park beside the Brooklyn Bridge.

"This is one of my favorite places." He took my hand and tugged me forward.

"I don't think I've ever been here before."

"Really?" He looked over at me. "I thought that everyone's been here."

"I haven't actually spent much time in the city." I shrugged. "When I'm not in school I spend a lot of time with my grandmother and when everyone else goes out, I usually hang back to study."

"Why?" He brushed my hair back from my eyes as he looked into them. "Why are you always hiding out?"

"I don't really think of it as hiding out."

"But it is." He led me down a slight slope to a grassy open area.

"I guess in a way—I guess I've learned to like the quiet."

"It's hard to find in a city that doesn't sleep." He sat down in the grass, then reached his hand up to me. "Want to join me?"

"Sure." I smiled as I sat down beside him. The grass was just a little damp and the sky above us painted with the lights of the city, brewed with clouds that promised a chance of rain.

"I come here a lot." He chewed on his lip. "Even though I'm not supposed to."

"Why not?" I rested my head on his shoulder and continued to study the sky.

"It's hard to explain."

"I feel like you know this city better than anyone I've ever met, but you act like you're not allowed in any part of it. I know I'm not supposed to ask questions, but isn't there anything that you can tell me about it?"

"Let's just say that I didn't commit any crimes, but I'm basically a prisoner." He shook his head and laughed a little. "Okay, maybe a few crimes, but that's not why I'm a prisoner."

"So that big scary reputation you have is just smoke?"

"Not exactly." He met my eyes. "I didn't take to being a prisoner too well. I'm used to being free. I'm used to being able to roam wherever I want, with anyone I want to. But when all that changed, I may have lost my temper a few times—acted out." He looked down at the grass that stuck up between his feet.

"And now?" I didn't dare to look at him. "Am I just part of that?"

"No." He caught the fingers of my hand that draped over the knee closest to him and gave them a light tug. "You're the reason I don't feel so angry anymore."

"I like that." I smiled. "I like being that reason."

"I like it too." He sprawled out across the grass and looked up at the sky.

I hesitated for a moment, then stretched out beside him.

He shifted his arm beneath me and guided my head to rest on his chest.

It felt a little awkward at first—the shifting and the uncertainty of what he wanted—but the moment my cheek touched his chest, a warmth washed over me that made me feel as if it was the only place I was ever meant to be. I listened to the sound of his heartbeat as his fingers wandered through the length of my hair.

For a second, I wondered if I was dreaming. I'd waited so long to feel this kind of connection with someone, but it still felt so tenuous.

"I don't want you to have to be angry anymore." I draped my arm across his stomach.

"I wish it could be that way." He drew a deep breath. "When this all started, it was supposed to be temporary. Now it feels like it will be forever."

"Whatever it is, Nicholas, I want you to know that I understand. I might not know, but I do understand that it's something in your life that you can't control. I spent a lot of my life wishing I could control things, shape my family into exactly what I wanted it to be. But the truth is we can't. People are going to be who they are." I tilted my head some to look up at him. "You don't have to tell me, but I know that whatever it is isn't your fault."

"It kind of is." He kissed the top of my head, then twirled his fingers through my hair some more. "Let's not talk about it."

"We don't have to." I bit into my bottom lip. The truth was, I wanted to talk about it. I wanted to know everything there was to know about him. But he'd made it clear that I couldn't push him.

As his fingers drifted from my hair, they caressed the curve of my arm, then ran right back up to my shoulder. His touch made my heart race. I felt his arms tighten around me again. We hadn't even kissed, but it felt as if our bodies were getting to know each other just by being close.

I closed my eyes and tried to resist the urge to lean up and press my lips against his. I didn't want to pressure him, not when I knew how delicate things were between us.

Take it slow, Candy, I reminded myself. Just let him make the first move when he's comfortable. But resisting my desire was new to me—and difficult.

Suddenly he shifted his body so that my head drifted to his arm. He pushed himself up on his elbow and looked down at me.

I gazed up at him. My heart slammed against my chest as his face hovered over mine.

He remained silent as he stared into my eyes. Then his fingertips traced the curve of my cheek.

I shivered at the sensation.

He smiled and ran his fingers down the other side of my cheek.

"What are you doing?" I smiled as I looked at him.

"Remembering you." His fingertips wandered across my chin, then traced lightly across my lips.

"You don't have to remember, I'm right here." My heart skipped a beat at the notion.

A small part of me wondered if I'd wandered into his web. Could any of this be real? He said the things I wanted to hear, things I thought I might never hear.

"I don't ever want to forget." He coasted his palm along my forehead, then cupped my cheek and leaned a little closer to me. "Where did you come from, Candace?"

"Nowhere special." I shrugged and held my breath as his lips inched just a little closer to mine.

"I don't believe that for a second." He smiled.

"It's true." I locked my eyes to his. "I'm just a girl, like any other girl you know."

"Not a chance." He shook his head. "You blow me away, you know that? Just by looking at me."

TWENTY-TWO

I swallowed hard. I wanted to say that he did the same, but the words stuck in my throat. I could only stare up at him and wish that he would lean just a little closer.

"Can we stay here?" His breath drifted with the faintest touch against my face.

"Right here." I whispered in return.

"Just us," he added, his eyes still locked to mine.

"Just us," I repeated and lifted my head enough to almost touch my lips to his.

He drew back just before they could meet, then smiled. "Not yet."

"Now?" I smiled.

"Not yet." He grinned, then planted a light kiss on my forehead. "I want to know that when I kiss you, it won't be the last time."

"It won't be."

"You don't know that." He winced.

I wrapped my arms around him and pulled him down on top of me. Instead of kissing him, I brushed my cheek across his and held him close. I understood then that he was afraid. I wasn't sure of exactly what, but it didn't matter. I wanted to hold him until he felt safe.

He buried his lips through my hair to the warmth of my neck, then rolled me over until I was on top of him.

As my hair dragged through the grass, the subtle tug was enough to bring me back to reality. His arms tightened around me and we stayed like that, wrapped up in each other for hours. I could only tell how much time had passed by the lightening of the sky. The lighter it became, the more anxious I became. I knew our moment couldn't last forever.

I'd just started to drift off to sleep, when Nicholas pressed his lips against my cheek and shifted his arm around me.

"Don't fade on me now. We're going to have to get back before daylight."

"No, we can stay here." I nestled closer to him. "Can't we?"

"I wish we could." He sighed as he leaned his head back in the grass. "I never expected to be out here all night with you."

"Neither did I." I closed my eyes as another wave of exhaustion washed over me.

"No, no, you can't go to sleep." He stroked my cheek until I opened my eyes. "I have to get you back safe and sound. Let's go. Up. On your feet." He jumped to his feet and reached his hand down to me.

I hesitated. I didn't want the night to end. I wanted it to last as long as possible. But as he smiled down at me, I took his hand and let him pull me to my feet. I rocked forward in the process and fell against his chest for just a second. Caught up in the scent of him, I was tempted yet again to kiss him.

"Sit over here for a minute." He guided me to a nearby bench, then sat down beside me. "We can have a few more minutes."

"It's pretty here." I pulled my feet up onto the bench and gazed out over the water.

"It is." He draped his arm across my shoulders.

In the middle of the busy city, the park gave some solace from the fast pace that surrounded it. But it was his warmth that calmed me. I had a million questions running through my mind, but I couldn't focus on any of them while his arm gave off the perfect amount of heat. I felt myself turn into his side just a little, inviting a connection I wasn't sure whether I could resist.

I knew I didn't want to resist. I thought about Ethan's attempt to kiss me earlier that evening. I'd pulled away so swiftly without the slightest hesitation. I hadn't had time to decide whether or not to kiss him. It had been pure instinct to evade the attempt.

With Nicholas, it was just the opposite. I craved his kiss much the way I might crave jumping into a cool stream on a blistering hot day. It was as if I couldn't experience relief until it happened.

He curved his body closer to mine and his chin rested on the top of my head.

I could feel it in the tension of his muscles as his arms tightened around me. I could hear it in his uneven breaths. He wanted the kiss as much as I did, but neither of us dared to admit it.

"You should get back." He trailed his fingertips along the curve of my hand.

"I don't want to."

"You should still get back, though." He shifted a little, so that my head drifted down further along his shoulder and came to rest against his chest.

"I want to stay right here."

"For a little while."

"Until the sun rises."

"Candace."

"You can call me Candy you know." I smiled, then tilted my head some to look up at him. "And maybe I can call you Nico."

His jaw tensed as he looked out across the park. "You probably shouldn't."

"It's your name, isn't it?" I wrapped my hand around his. "I heard that cop call you that. Nico."

"Yeah." He sighed. "But you shouldn't call me that."

"Why not?" I frowned, then closed my eyes. "Never mind, forget I asked that. I promised to leave you with your secrets."

"I know it isn't fair. I wish it wasn't like this."

"I don't care how it is. I'm just happy to be here with you." I reached up and caressed his cheek. "Whatever happened to make your life such a mystery, Nico, I'm sorry."

"I said don't call me that." He sat me up and looked into my eyes. "You can't call me that. Do you understand?"

"I'm sorry, it was just a slip-up." I frowned.

"That's the thing. There can't be any slip-ups." He cupped my cheeks and gazed into my eyes. For a split-second I thought he might kiss me finally. His thumbs stroked my cheeks. His lips moved as if they hungered for things that there were no words for. But his eyes narrowed and his voice sharpened. "I can't do this."

"What?"

His hands fell away from my cheeks and he stood up from the bench. "I can't do this. Do you hear me?"

"I hear you, but I don't believe you." I stood up as well. "You said we could try. You said we could keep it our secret, that it could just be us."

"I know what I said!" He ran his hands through his hair and turned away from me. "I wish you could just stop! Just stop for one second!"

"Stop what?" My heart pounded with panic. "Just tell me what you want me to do and I'll do it. I promise!"

"You can't!" He turned back, his eyes wild as he looked at me. "You can't do it, because you can't stop being you. I look at you and I can't think anymore! You speak and it's the only thing I can hear. Don't you see?"

"I do." I grabbed his hand and held it tight. "I feel it too, Nicholas, I know how powerful it is."

"Then you should understand!" He twisted his hand until I released it. "This can't happen. It just can't."

"It can if we let it. That's all we have to do. Remember?" I tried to meet his eyes, desperate to be reassured that he wasn't about to ruin everything.

"It's a lie. It's all pretend. What I have with you isn't pretend. I can't put you in danger. I care about you too much to do that."

"In danger of what?" I laughed. "Of actually, finally, having a real connection with someone?"

"Go home, Candy." He took a step back from me and held his hands out in front of him. "Please. If you care about me at all, you'll drop this. We need to both let it go."

"I won't!" I stared at him, my eyes wide. "I won't! Do you hear me? I'm not going to let this go! I'm not going to let the best part of my life just disappear because you're too scared!"

"I am scared!" He shouted. "I'm scared and I should be. I'm scared for you. I will do absolutely anything to protect you. Do you understand that?"

"Not this!" I glared at him. "You're not protecting me! You're tearing me apart!"

"I'm sorry." He reached for me, then drew his hand back a second later. "I'm sorry, Candy, but this is how it has to be. You're going to have to deal with that." He turned and started to walk away.

"Don't you dare! Don't walk away from me!" I held my breath as I waited for him to turn back. It would be the perfect time for him to pull me into his arms and kiss me with more passion than I could even imagine.

Instead, he continued to walk.

I stood there, frozen to the ground by my own horror. After the amazing night we'd spent together, how could all of it be coming to an end? Briefly I considered the possibility of chasing after him. I could demand that he look at me. I could call him a coward and accuse him of not being strong enough to make it work. But I resisted the urge.

If he could walk away, then it was very simple. He didn't feel about me the way I felt about him. I had to face it and move on from it. I knew it would take some time, but I would find a way to get over it. I had no other choice.

TWENTY-THREE

As I slipped back through the fence at Oak Brook, I wished that I'd never gone through it in the first place. I wanted more than anything to forget that I'd ever met Nicholas. He'd spun my life around in just the short time that he'd been part of it, then ripped away any sense of magic and love that I'd discovered. To me, it was far more cruel than never having felt it at all.

As I looked in the direction of the courtyard, I knew that I couldn't go back to my dorm room. I couldn't face Apple. I couldn't face anyone. Instead, I shifted direction and headed for the hideout.

As I approached, a heard some sounds from inside. Yes, someone was there, but I didn't care. It was the only place I had to go, the only place where I could safely explode.

I burst through the door and slammed it shut behind me. The anger that flowed through me was more intense than anything I'd ever experienced before. "Never again!"

"Candy?" Jenny nearly fell off Gabriel's lap. He caught her just before she could hit the floor. "What's wrong?"

"Everything." I tossed myself onto the pillows piled on the

floor. So soft and yet so firm. They reminded me of lying against Nicholas's chest. I began to punch them.

"Candy?" Jenny walked over to me and frowned. "Hon, what happened?"

"I don't want to talk about it." My chest burned as I did my best to ignore Gabriel's presence.

Another man. Would he hurt Jenny the way that Nicholas insisted on hurting me? I doubted it. They'd been so hot and heavy ever since they'd hooked up. Unlike mine, their romance had actually gone somewhere. It seemed to me that they'd gotten a lot further than a first kiss.

"This is about Nicholas, isn't it?" Jenny frowned as she sprawled out beside me.

"Want me to knock him out for you?" Gabriel took off his guitar and set it against the wall.

"Would you?" I peered up at him, then sighed. "No. I'm the one that's being ridiculous, not him. I'm sorry I interrupted you guys. Will you play something for me? I need some kind of distraction before my brain explodes."

"I know that feeling." Jenny hugged me. "Sure, we can play for you." She stifled a yawn, then pushed herself to her feet. "But I'll be honest with you. A distraction isn't going to solve anything. When it comes down to it, you're going to have to figure out what's really gotten under your skin about this guy."

"What do you mean?" I sat up and looked at her as my heart pounded. I realized that Jenny was dangerously close to knowing the truth about things between me and Nicholas, which according to him could be very dangerous. I had to make sure that she didn't know too much. "He's a royal jerk. That's what's gotten under my skin."

"Sure." Gabriel strummed his guitar.

"You stay out of this!" I hurled a pillow at him.

"Watch the guitar!" He huffed, then shook his head. "All

I'm saying is that you two manage to spend a lot of time together for two people that can't stand each other."

"I don't care what anyone says." I stood up and placed my hands on my hips. "There is no way I would ever even look twice at that fool. We got stuck together and every time I think there's anything decent about him, he goes ahead and proves me wrong."

"Alright, we've got the picture." Jenny wrapped her arms around me. "Don't worry, you're going to get through this. Gabriel, play."

"Your wish is my command." He winked at Jenny, then began to strum the guitar.

I rested my head against Jenny's shoulder and closed my eyes. I felt her pluck something from my hair.

I opened my eyes to see a few blades of grass pinched between her fingers.

"What exactly were you two doing until dawn?" She raised an eyebrow.

"Sh." I buried my face into her shoulder. "Just sing."

I trembled with the memory of Nicholas's arms around me, the grass beneath us, the warm soil against my skin. I knew that Jenny was right about how I felt about Nicholas. I also knew that it didn't matter. There wouldn't be any happy ending to my story.

As the song came to an end, I noticed the way that Jenny and Gabriel stared at one another. That heat—that was what I felt when I looked at Nicholas. So why was it right for them, but out of reach for me? I shuddered again and closed my eyes.

"Everything's going to be just fine." Jenny squeezed me, then smiled. "I'm going to help you get through this. I promise."

"Can you get him kicked out?" I lifted my head enough to look at her.

She smiled. "Let's just figure out exactly what you want

first." She brushed my hair back from my eyes. "Then we'll figure out a plan to get it."

"Thank you." I hugged her again.

She helped me to my feet, then walked me to the door. As I stepped outside, I glanced over my shoulder and heard the two exchange "I love yous."

Just a few days ago that was all I wanted. Someone to share that kind of connection with. But everything had changed since then. Now I wanted Nicholas and I wasn't sure that I could be satisfied with anything else. Whose fault was that?

"It's his fault." I threw my hand in the air as Jenny walked beside me.

"Whose fault?"

"Nicholas's." I crossed my arms. "I had zero interest in him. He's the one that started flirting with me."

"I think that's just his natural reaction to being around a girl." Jenny winced.

I bit into my bottom lip. I knew that I'd wandered dangerously close to the edge of confessing my feelings for Nicholas. But I needed to talk to someone. I needed to get it out once and for all.

"I'm sorry, I shouldn't have interrupted you two."

"Don't be sorry." Jenny glanced at me as we reached the dormitories. "Just tell me the truth. Where were you last night?"

"Brooklyn." I met her eyes.

"With Nicholas?"

My heart pounded as I tried to fight the sensation that hearing his name created.

"With a few people. Yes, Nicholas was there too."

"Do you have some kind of crush on him?" Jenny frowned.

"No, of course not. It's just—well, he can be a little confusing. Like you said, he flirts with everyone. I guess I just took it a little too seriously."

"I don't think you're telling me the whole truth." She opened the door to the girls' dormitory. "You can tell me, you know."

"I don't even want to think about it anymore." I sighed. "All that matters is that he isn't part of my life. And it's going to stay that way."

"That's probably a good thing." She met my eyes. "The things I've heard about him...Candy, he's not the right guy for you."

I knew that she meant her words to be kind, but they only hurt. I forced a nod, then fled up the stairs to my dorm room.

When I reached it, the tears began to flow.

Was I really the only one that could see us together? Was I so boring—so plain—that a boy like him could never like a girl like me?

I was about to step into my bedroom when there was a sharp knock at the door.

"Jenny, I told you, I don't want to talk about it." I threw the door open and frowned. My eyes widened at the sight of one of the dorm monitors, Gina, with one of the security guards.

"Candace, when did you return to your dorm?" Gina crossed her arms.

TWENTY-FOUR

"Last night." I mumbled the words.

"Really? Then how come I saw you sneaking around outside the fence an hour ago?" The security guard pulled out his phone.

"I went for a walk..." I bit into my bottom lip.

"Through a gap in the fence?" He held up his phone and displayed a picture that he'd taken of me sneaking back in.

My heart hammered against my chest as I watched both of them narrow their eyes. No, there wasn't any getting out of this one.

"Every year you sign an agreement to follow the rules, don't you, Candace?" Gina gestured for me to step out into the hallway.

"Yes, I do." I stepped out into the hall and watched as the security guard walked off.

"Then you agree that you've committed a violation of those rules?" She opened the folder she held in her hand.

"Yes." I closed my eyes as my mind spun with all the possibilities. "Please don't expel me."

"That's not up to me. You need to report to the principal's

office." She handed me a slip of paper. "Before classes start, otherwise you're going to have another violation."

"Okay, I will. I'm just going to change and then I'll go right there."

"Might want to shower too." She plucked a piece of grass from my hair.

Mortified, I stepped back into the dorm room.

Apple stared at me sleepily from the doorway of her bedroom. "What's going on? Is everything okay?"

"It's fine." I clenched my teeth. How would I ever tell my friends that I'd messed up this bad? And over a guy who clearly didn't care about me the way I cared about him?

It was ridiculous. As I washed off in the shower, I tried to wash away my feelings for him too. But each time I brushed the soap from my skin, I remembered the stroke of his fingertips. When the warm water rushed over my body, I remembered how warm I'd felt with his arms wrapped around me.

As I dressed, I thought about the texture of his shirt that my cheek had rested against.

By the time I arrived at the principal's office, my stomach was in knots from my desire and my frustration with him. He'd gone from snuggling close to me all night to telling me that he couldn't see me again. How was I supposed to just accept that?

As I sat down across from the principal, I realized that I had more important matters to attend to.

"Candace." He frowned as he looked across his desk at me. "What's going on with you lately?"

"Sir?"

"I see that you recently had weekend detention and now you've been caught off campus after curfew?" He shook his head. "It doesn't seem like you."

"I'm very sorry, sir. I know there's no excuse. If you would please consider allowing me to stay, I can assure you that nothing like this will ever happen again." I forced myself to look into his eyes.

"I'm not sure if I can believe that." He sat back in his chair and folded his hands on the center of his chest. "Candace, we here at Oak Brook Academy pride ourselves on offering not just an exceptional education, but a safe and welcoming environment. I can't promise that safety to your fellow students if you aren't following the rules, now can I?"

"It was a very bad decision on my part."

"One you made alone?" He locked his eyes to mine.

"What?"

"Perhaps you'd like to tell me who showed you the hole in the fence."

My heart skipped a beat. "I just found it."

"Lying is not going to help your case, Candace." He sat forward and placed his hands on his desk between us. "Now, if you'd like to tell me the truth, I might consider some leniency. The question is, how important is being a student here at Oak Brook Academy to you?"

My chest tightened. Oak Brook was more than just my school. It was my family. It was my home, when even home didn't really feel like home. It had been the one stable thing in my life for the past few years. How could I even consider allowing myself to be expelled?

"Candace?" He looked into my eyes.

"I can't." My heart sank as I closed my eyes.

"Candace, it's my belief that someone cut a hole in that fence. I would like to make sure that person is punished for his act. But I can't do that if you're not going to tell me who it was. If you really want to stay here and you respect the rules of Oak Brook Academy, then you'll tell me who did this. It's the only way we can ensure the safety of every student here."

I couldn't tell the truth, could I? Nicholas would be in so much trouble.

Suddenly I wondered why I cared. He had been the one to show me the hole in the fence. He had been the one to encourage me to be out after curfew. Why shouldn't I tell the truth? Clearly all he wanted was to toy with me. He'd success-fully lured me and shattered my heart. So why shouldn't I let him feel some consequences for his own actions?

"Candace, this is the last time I'm going to ask you." The principal tapped his fingers against the desk. "You have to make a decision here. Are you going to take the fall for someone else or are you going to prove to me that you really want to be a part of Oak Brook Academy?"

"Nicholas." I blurted the name out before I could lose my nerve. "Nicholas Holden."

"Nicholas?" He sighed and sat back in his chair. "Of course it's Nicholas." He pressed a button on his phone and spoke into it. "Please find me Nicholas Holden and get him in here right away."

I squirmed in my chair. My heart threatened to rip into pieces. Had I really just betrayed the only person I'd ever come close to falling in love with? Had I thrown him under a bus when I knew his situation was dangerous?

Only I didn't know that. I didn't know why his situation was dangerous. For all I knew, he could have made up the entire story just to coax me out for the night. Maybe he thought I'd fawn all over him—that he'd get what he wanted, then have an excuse not to speak to me again.

Only he hadn't done that.

I touched my cheek as I remembered his touch. He hadn't tried to take advantage of me at all.

I began to feel some panic deep within me as I wondered what I would say to him. How would I explain this?

The office door swung open. I heard his voice before I saw him.

"You wanted to see me, sir?"

Every muscle in my body tightened as I braced myself for his reaction. How angry would he be when he found out what I'd told the principal? I forced myself not to look at him as he stepped further into the office.

"You don't look very well rested, Nicholas." The principal gestured to the chair beside mine. "Please, sit down and tell me where you've been all night."

Nicholas eased himself down into the chair. His elbow brushed mine as he settled back into it. "Is this a trick question?"

"It's just a question." The principal shrugged. "Is there a reason you're hesitant to answer it?"

I felt him look at me. I felt the pressure of his attention as it lingered on the side of my face. I ducked my head a little further, allowing a bit of my hair to fall forward.

"I was in Brooklyn." He didn't look away from me as he spoke. "But I guess you already know that."

TWENTY-FIVE

"What am I going to do with you, Nicholas?" Principal Carter stared at him. "I understand that we have an agreement, but that agreement doesn't allow you to continually break our rules."

"Sir, I just needed to spend some time away." Nicholas shrugged and shifted his arm so that his forearm nearly touched mine. "It won't happen again."

"I'm sure it won't happen again." He glanced from Nicholas to me, then back again. "Are you the reason there's been such a change in Candace's behavior?"

"No." I spoke up before Nicholas could answer. "No, he has nothing to do with any of this."

"I find that hard to believe." The principal cleared his throat. "Alright, enough of this discussion. I want both of you in detention after school today."

I winced at the thought. Not only was I in trouble, but I was going to be stuck with Nicholas again? I couldn't imagine how cold he would be to me after the trouble I'd caused.

"We'll be there." Nicholas stood up from his chair.

"Actually, sir, if it wouldn't be too much of a problem,

maybe I could serve my detention at lunch or before school?" I dug my fingernails into the arm of the chair.

"That's not how detention works, Candace. You need to be where I say when I say. After school. Got it?" He looked into my eyes.

"Just for today?" I frowned. I could make it through one day. I was sure of it.

"For the remainder of the week and next week as well." He sighed. "I know you may think I'm being harsh about this, but the thought that the two of you were off wandering through the city in the middle of the night—well, it just terrifies me. Anything could have happened. It's just not safe. At your age, danger doesn't seem real; I get that." He looked sternly at Nicholas. "You especially should have been more cautious. I'm afraid I'm going to have to notify your father about this."

"Sir, please reconsider." Nicholas stepped closer to his desk. "It was a mistake. I'll do the detention. I'll even do more if you want. But I don't want to add any more stress to my father's life right now."

"I'll bet you don't." The principal looked up at him. "But it's my duty to keep him informed and that's exactly what I'm going to do."

"Fine." Nicholas turned and pushed his way back out through the door.

When I heard the door snap shut I took a sharp breath. A part of me was relieved that he'd left without saying a word to me. But I couldn't help but wonder if that meant he was too furious to look at me or if he'd already forgotten that I existed.

"Candace, you don't have to tell me what you were doing with Nicholas last night." Mr. Carter frowned as he straightened some papers on his desk. "But it would be best if you focused your attention on other boys, I think."

"Yes, sir." My cheeks flushed as I did my best to endure the advice on my love life from a man whom I'd feared and respected ever since I'd arrived at Oak Brook.

Humiliated, I stepped out of the office and into the hallway. Hot tears bit at my eyes. I squeezed them shut and took a shaky breath. Not only had I betrayed Nicholas, but I'd embarrassed myself in front of the principal. I had almost two weeks of detention to look forward to and a very angry call from my grandmother in my future.

Even worse, within a few hours I would be face to face with Nicholas. At least I would have a little time to get my story straight. Or maybe I could still find my way out of it.

I turned down the hall to head to my first class of the day. As I passed by an empty classroom, the door swung open and someone grabbed me by the arm.

"Hey!" I jerked my arm free as I turned to look at my assailant. "Nicholas." I gasped as I took a step back.

He grabbed my arm again. His eyes locked to mine as he tugged me into the classroom.

My heart raced, not out of fear, but out of exhilaration, which only confused me more.

He released my arm and pushed the door closed, then walked across the room to the bank of windows that faced the courtyard.

I lingered by the door, tempted to pull it open and disappear. I watched as he leaned his hands against the windowsill and stared out through the glass. The sunlight played against his skin, leaving behind patches of gold. As much as I wanted to hate him, all I could feel was an urge to wrap my arms around him.

"Nicholas, I'm sorry."

He turned to face me and leaned back against the windowsill. "For what?"

"Don't make me say it." I frowned.

"You're sorry for turning me in?" He walked toward me.

"Yes." I lowered my eyes. "I'm sorry. I shouldn't have said anything. I'm sure I've gotten you into all kinds of trouble." As I stared at the floor his shoes came into view. He stood about a foot away from me.

"Yes, you have."

"I'm sorry." I closed my eyes.

"Candy." His fingertips touched the bottom of my chin and guided it upward.

My eyes fluttered open and instantly connected with his. He didn't look angry. Not even a little.

"I am in so much trouble," he whispered as he continued to look into my eyes.

The first bell rang out in the hallway.

My heart lurched.

"We're going to be late."

"Don't go." He trailed his thumb along the curve of my chin. "Stay here with me."

"I can't." My mind raced as I wondered why he would ask me to stay after telling me to go not long before. "Nicholas, you have to believe me. I didn't mean to cause you any trouble."

"I believe you." He smiled as he let his hand fall away. "But here we are."

"I'll talk to the principal. I'll try to stop him from calling your father."

He shook his head, then reached past me to open the classroom door. "That's not the trouble I'm worried about." He tipped his head toward the crowd of students in the hallway. "Better hurry, wouldn't want you to be stuck with me any longer than you have to be."

"Nicholas." I reached for his hand.

"I'm dangerous, remember?" He took a step back and locked

his eyes to mine. "Get to class, Candy, before I cause you even more trouble."

As my eyes lingered on his, I understood exactly what he meant. Being late for class wasn't the trouble I was worried about. The trouble that swept over me the moment he smiled at me was the ache in my chest and the dizziness in my head.

I turned and stepped into the rush of students. When I glanced back over my shoulder, Nicholas was gone.

The memory of his touch caused my skin to tingle all through my first class. I tried to force my thoughts away from him. I tried to focus on my studies. But every few seconds my mind wandered back to the way he'd smiled at me. I expected him to be furious, to never want anything to do with me again. Instead, he'd acted like he didn't care at all about the principal or his punishment.

At lunch, I headed for the library. I needed some time to think and being surrounded by my well-meaning friends wouldn't help with that. I knew that they wouldn't understand the strange web that I'd stumbled into.

Nicholas didn't think we should be together—he'd made that clear—but was he the only one who had a say in the matter?

I grabbed a few snacks from the vending machine and settled at a table with one of my favorite books. But the words only swam across the page.

"Hey, beautiful." A hand settled on my shoulder.

TWENTY-SIX

I glanced over my shoulder expecting to see Nicholas. Instead, Ethan smiled at me as he slid into the chair beside me.

"Sorry if I startled you. I thought you would be at lunch, and when you weren't, Apple suggested that you might be here." He met my eyes. "I hope you aren't trying to avoid me, or this will be very awkward."

I bit into my bottom lip. I could have told him that I was trying to avoid the entire world, not just him, but I didn't think he would understand that.

I thought about the way that Nicholas had pulled me into the classroom after the meeting with the principal. What was all that supposed to mean? It didn't change anything. He still didn't think we should be together. A part of me wondered too if it was too much of a risk to be with him. I had no idea what his secrets were, but whatever they were, he certainly wasn't ready to share them with me.

It seemed to me that he could turn things on and off pretty easily. Me, on the other hand? When I looked into his eyes, I thought I might drown. He obviously didn't feel the same way. That afternoon was going to be challenging, to say the least.

But here was Ethan. Here was a distraction. Someone who could prove that I wasn't hung up on a guy whom I couldn't possibly be with.

"No, I wasn't trying to avoid you." I offered a small smile. "I'm just very tired."

"Didn't sleep well?" He peered at the cover of my book.

"Something like that." I held up the book. "One of my favorites. Have you read it?"

"I don't think so." He shrugged. "I'm more into sci-fi than fantasy."

"Any favorites?"

"Probably not anything that you would have read." He pulled out his phone. "So, I was thinking. There's this walk tonight with the astronomy club."

"Oh, you're in the astronomy club?" I smiled.

"No, but my friend is, and he said we'd blend in easily if we wanted to go with them. What do you say? Wouldn't it be nice for our first date to be under the stars?" He looked into my eyes.

"Our first date?" My chest tightened.

"Yes, okay, this is my awkward way of asking." He ruffled his hand through his hair. "You don't have to say yes. I know I tried to move things a little too fast yesterday and I'm sorry about that." He frowned. "I guess I was just trying to be someone else."

"It's okay." I managed a smile. "A walk under the stars sounds really nice. I appreciate you thinking of me. But I have detention."

"Detention?" He laughed. "You're joking, right?"

"No." My cheeks flushed. "Unfortunately, no."

"What could you have possibly done to get detention?" His eyes widened.

I stared at him. A week before, I would have agreed with him.

A week ago, I wasn't someone who would get detention. But all of that had changed. Now I was someone who slipped through holes in fences, who hung out on the top of the Brooklyn Bridge, who rode in the back of a police car and stayed up all night in the arms of a guy I didn't have a chance of being with.

Only that old me? That me was confused and hurt and lonely. I didn't want to be that me.

"It was a misunderstanding." I rolled my eyes. "But what can I do? You know."

"Maybe I could talk to someone for you? Principal Carter?"

"You think you could get me out of it?" I grinned.

"I could try." He smiled.

"Don't worry about it. I'll just do my time. I'll catch up on some reading."

"Is it because of Nicholas?" He met my eyes. "Is he the reason that you have detention?"

"No." I glanced away. "It has nothing to do with him. We're not even friends."

"Alright, well, you can still come tonight if you want to. The bus doesn't leave until after dinner. You'll be done with detention." He shrugged. "If you want to."

"I do." I closed my book. "I'll be there, Ethan. Thanks for inviting me."

"I'm looking forward to it." He smiled at me then stood up from the table. "See you tonight."

As I watched him leave the library, I waited for some kind of desire to stir within me. He was nice enough and those dimples in his cheeks certainly made him endearing. So why couldn't I just like him the way he liked me?

Maybe because I'd let myself get too caught up in my feelings for Nicholas.

I promised myself that I would actually go on the date with

Ethan. I wouldn't just pretend. I would enjoy his company and if he tried to kiss me, I wasn't going to dodge it.

I needed to get Nicholas off my mind. Ethan was a great way to do that. So was finding out the truth about Nicholas.

If things were as bad as everyone seemed to think, then I couldn't possibly continue to want to be with him. But there weren't a lot of ways to find out that information. All I knew for sure was that he was somehow connected with the police and that no one wanted him anywhere near me. He had another name or at least another name he went by—one that I wasn't allowed to speak. The principal seemed to be aware of his situation, as he mentioned an agreement with Nicholas's father.

So, what was the big secret? I'd promised him that I would let him keep it, but that was when I thought he would give us a chance. Now that I knew he wouldn't, I was determined to find out why.

If there was one person at Oak Brook Academy who always knew everything about everyone, it was Maby. She'd been sketchy about Nicholas from the start, which was unusual for her. She didn't judge people and usually encouraged her friends to keep an open mind. But she felt differently about Nicholas for some reason.

I packed up my book and headed back toward the cafeteria. It didn't take me long to spot Maby huddled under a tree with her arms around Oliver. The pair had been inseparable lately.

"Maby?" I paused beside them and waited for their lips to untangle. "Sorry to interrupt."

"It's fine." Maby grinned as she gave Oliver a playful shove. "Girl talk."

"Seriously? You're just going to toss me aside?" He slid his arm around her waist and pulled her back in for another kiss.

I did my best not to roll my eyes. Sure, it was sweet, but I was impatient.

"Alright, enough." Maby laughed as she pushed him away again. "Go on, Candy and I need to have a chat." As she locked her eyes to mine, I sensed that she had a lot to say.

Oliver gave us both a wave then walked off to join a group of boys near the football field.

"I was hoping to catch you at lunch." Maby leaned back against the tree as she looked at me. "I heard about you getting caught."

"That's not what I need to talk about."

"It should be." She frowned. "Your reputation is important, Candy. You can't let it get messed up over Nicholas."

"Why not?" I crossed my arms. "What's so bad about him?"

"I knew you weren't over him." She sighed.

"I am." I glared at her. "I'm completely over him. But I just don't understand what the big secret is. What's so terrible about him?"

"I don't know anything." Maby shoved her hands into her pockets.

"Now you're lying to me?" I shook my head. "I thought we were better friends than that."

"Candy." She lowered her voice. "I've told you, this is just not something you want to get in the middle of, okay?"

TWENTY-SEVEN

"No, it's not okay." I stepped closer to her. "I'm done being told what is good for me and what isn't. I'm done with other people making my choices for me. I want to know the truth about Nicholas, and if you can't tell me that, then we were never actually friends, were we?"

My heart raced as anger flooded through me. I'd never spoken to Maby like this. I knew she didn't deserve it. But I was desperate and frustrated and I needed her to be honest.

"We are friends." Maby stared straight into my eyes. "Always. But what you're asking for isn't about friendship. It's about danger."

"Tell me." I frowned. "Tell me or I'm done with you and with the whole crew. If you can't trust me enough to tell me the truth, then I don't belong in your circle of friends."

"That's enough." Maby held up one finger and stared straight at me. "You know how much I care about you and you know that our friendship is unshakable. So, drop the nonsense, got it?"

"Maby!" I groaned. "How is that I'm the one who has to be

kept in the dark? If you know something, how is it fair for you to keep it to yourself?"

She glanced around us, then tugged me closer to the side of the building. She lowered her voice and leaned close to me. "The kind of people that are looking for Nicholas are ruthless. Alright?"

"What? Why is anyone looking for him?"

"I can't tell you everything. I don't know everything. All I know are things that I've picked up from rumors and conversations I've overheard—particularly between Nicholas's father and Principal Carter." She frowned. "I don't know the whole story. All I know is that Nicholas is here not just for an education, but for his protection."

"You said you overheard a conversation between the principal and Nicholas's father. That means you know who he is." I took a breath, then looked into her eyes. "Please, can you at least tell me that?"

"You have to swear you won't tell anyone. I mean it, Candy."

"I swear." I held up my hands. "I just want some idea of what is going on here. I don't want to do anything to hurt Nicholas."

"Nicholas's father is the police commissioner for all of New York City."

"Oh." My eyes widened. "That explains a lot."

"It does?"

"Yes. How the police know him so well and why he's so intimidated by his father."

"Now you know." Maby frowned. "But I'm not sure that I should have told you. Please, promise me you're going to stay away from him. I'd hate to see something happen to you just because you're standing next to him."

"Like I said, there's nothing between us." My heart

pounded. If Nicholas was in danger that would explain why he didn't want me near him. But why was he in danger? Just for being the son of the police commissioner? I doubted it. There had to be more to it than that.

Now that I knew who his father was, I could find out more about him.

"I wish I could believe that." Maby searched my eyes, then shook her head. "I know it can be hard when feelings are running strong, but it's for the best that you let this go. Ethan seems nice."

"Yes, he does." I nodded. "Thank you." I hugged her. "I appreciate you telling me the truth. I'm sorry for what I said."

"Yes, you were ready to walk away from our friendship, but you don't have any feelings for Nicholas, right?" She smiled some as she pulled away from my hug. "I'm not the one lying now."

"I'm going to stay away from him." I narrowed my eyes. "Obviously, he didn't trust me enough to tell me the truth. That's pretty telling, don't you think?"

"All I know is that he's been trying to get kicked out of this place ever since he arrived. I guess nobody consulted him about this decision. I'm sure it can't be easy for him. But that doesn't excuse his behavior. He flirts with every girl he sees and he's gotten you into all kinds of trouble. Just take my advice and make sure you keep your distance."

"I will." I bit into my bottom lip. I would—at least after I finished serving detention with him.

Armed with more knowledge than I'd ever had about him, I went through my afternoon classes full of determination. I would do my time with Nicholas. I would be polite, but I would resist the urge to be drawn into the chaos that was my feelings for him. I would focus instead on the perfectly romantic date I had with Ethan that evening.

If a stroll under the stars couldn't stir enough romance to satisfy me, then clearly, I was the problem.

As I entered the library to serve my detention, I noticed Nicholas already seated at one of the tables. He had his phone out and a notebook open on the table in front of him.

The moment he looked up at me, I took a sharp breath. Just his eyes meeting mine was enough to knock the wind out of me. He stared for a long moment, then looked back down at his phone.

I walked over to a table on the other side of the room. I really would keep my distance.

He could have told me who his father was when we were in the back of the police car. He could have promised me that I didn't have to worry about being locked away. Instead, he'd let me sweat it out. He kept his secret, even though he didn't have to. That was the kind of person he was. The kind of person that I certainly didn't want to be with.

I flipped open my book and pretended to read. I slid my phone out of my pocket and hid it with my book. Maybe Nicholas could get away with playing on his phone in detention, but I was likely to get in big trouble for it. Now that I knew whose son he was, I could search for more information about him.

As I searched online, however, I came across mostly old articles. Information about the Little League team he played for. Stories about his parents' divorce and the custody battle that left him in his father's custody. Nothing about why he might be hidden away at Oak Brook Academy. Every article I read referred to him as Nico, but his legal name was listed as Nicholas.

"Find anything interesting?"

I jumped at the sound of his voice just above my shoulder. When my hands jerked, my phone slid out of my book and landed with a clatter against the table. I reached for it, but before I could grab it, he snatched it up.

My heart pounded as he began to read over the article open on the screen. It was about his father's latest move against gang violence.

"Doesn't look like your kind of reading." He glanced up from my phone and looked into my eyes. His voice was tight as he spoke. "Don't you have better things to be doing?"

"Give it back, Nico." I held my hand out to him. My cheeks burned as I realized what I'd called him. I'd been reading the name over and over again in the articles I'd found. It just slipped from my mouth without a second thought.

Nicholas passed a quick glance around us, then turned a stern glare on me. "You couldn't leave it alone? You couldn't just trust me?"

"You didn't trust me either." I snatched my phone back from his hand. "Did you?"

"What exactly do you know?" He pulled a chair over close to mine, then straddled it so that he could face me. "Tell me now."

"I don't have to tell you anything." I picked my book back up. "We're not supposed to talk during detention."

"Candy!" He pulled my book out of my hands and tossed it down on the table. "This isn't a game. You need to tell me everything you know."

His eyes burned into mine with such determination that I had to look away. Suddenly, I was frightened. Was he hidden away because he'd done something terrible? Was this some kind of cover-up to protect his father's reputation?

TWENTY-EIGHT

"Sh!" The librarian's sharp warning echoed through the otherwise quiet library.

I picked up my book and stared hard at the table.

Nicholas sank down into the chair beside me and grabbed the edge of my chair. He pulled the chair, with me on it, closer to him and lowered his voice to a stern whisper.

"This is very important, Candy. You need to tell me what you know."

"You first." I met his eyes.

"Candy."

"Nicholas. You keep saying this is important, but you're not willing to tell me why. So, no." I stood up from my chair. "I'm not going to tell you anything. Not until you tell me something —anything—that's real." I gathered my book and my bag as I waited for his response.

When I was met with silence, I looked into his eyes again. "No?"

"Candy, you don't understand."

"You're right, I don't. I know this is a very dangerous situation. I know that you feel you have to hide everything from me and I'm pretty sure that you've convinced yourself that it's all for my sake, but I'm not going to sit back and wait for you to tell me the truth anymore." I turned toward the door.

"Detention isn't over." He frowned as he stood up as well.

"It is for me." I walked right through the door and closed it behind me.

It wasn't until I was on the outside of the library that I realized just how much trouble I could get into for leaving detention early. As much as I wanted to be as far away from Nicholas as possible, I also didn't want to be expelled.

I considered going back into the library and serving out the rest of my sentence. But how could I face him again? I'd lost it and part of me knew that it wasn't terribly fair of me. Whatever Nicholas had to hide from, he probably had his reasons. But I was tired of not knowing.

I hurried back to my dorm room, prepared to be faced with another meeting with the principal. It stunned me as I realized that I felt more comfortable dealing with the principal and a possible expulsion than I did facing Nicholas again.

I sprawled out on my bed and squeezed my eyes shut tight. Just closing them wasn't enough to keep the memory of his touch out of my thoughts. It didn't matter that he didn't tell me the truth. I still had the same feelings for him. I imagined a switch I could turn off inside of me, something that would put an end to the anguish of thinking I would never get to be alone with him again.

I skipped dinner and stayed in my room instead. The thought of facing my friends made me uneasy. They all seemed to have everything together, while I felt as if I was falling apart. It wasn't until my phone began to ring that I even remembered my date with Ethan.

"Oh no!"

"Candy?" Apple knocked on my door. "Is everything okay in there?"

"What do you even wear for a date with the stars?"

"With the stars?" She lingered near the door. "Did you meet a celebrity? Are you going to some kind of red carpet party?"

"What? No! What are you talking about?" I began tearing clothes out of my closet. I needed Ethan to like me. I needed him to want to kiss me. I needed a spark between us to burn so bright that I would never think about Nicholas again.

"You're not making any sense." Apple sighed, then pulled open the door. "I thought you said you have a date with a star?"

"This?" I held up a silver sleeveless blouse. "Maybe it will sparkle in the stars?"

"Oh!" Apple laughed. "Are you going on the astronomy field trip?"

"Yes, Ethan asked me to go with him." I tossed the blouse down on my bed and picked up a black shirt. "How about this one?"

"I've never seen you like this." She frowned as she walked over to my closet. "You do realize that it's going to be dark, right? You need to focus more on texture. He might not be able to see you, but he'll be able to feel you."

"Oh, I didn't even think of that!" I groaned. "Is there anything in there that will work?"

"Perfect." Apple held up a soft sweater. "Just fuzzy enough to be enticing."

"Enticing? I'm not sure what is enticing about fuzzy, but I do love that sweater."

"Trust me, when he snuggles up to you in the dark, he's not going to want to let you go." Apple winked at me. "That's what you want isn't it?"

"Sure, yes of course." I smiled. "Thanks, Apple. I have to hurry."

I quickly changed in the bathroom, then rushed down the stairs and out into the courtyard.

As soon as I stepped outside, I felt a hand curl around mine.

"Candy, we need to talk." Nicholas met my eyes.

"No." I pulled my hand away just as Ethan waved to me from across the courtyard.

"Candy!" He smiled. "Are you ready? The bus is going to leave soon."

"I'll be right there." I forced a smile. "Just a second."

"We don't have a second." Ethan settled his gaze on Nicholas.

Suddenly I found myself caught between them—Ethan eager to dazzle me and Nicholas demanding my attention.

"I have to go." I glanced briefly at Nicholas and noticed the way his jaw tensed.

I forced myself to walk toward Ethan. I had to find a way to get over the draw that I felt toward Nicholas, even if it meant lying to myself to get me through it.

"Is everything okay?" Ethan frowned as he took my hand. "Was he bothering you?"

"No, we were just talking." I smiled. "Let's go check out those stars."

"Great." He brushed his free hand along the sleeve of my sweater, then grinned. "Wow, this is so soft."

My stomach twisted. Yes, the sweater was going to do the trick, but it wasn't enough to change the way I felt.

On the bus ride, Ethan wouldn't stop talking. I caught every fourth or fifth word. Enough to nod and smile when it seemed expected. But my thoughts kept drifting back to what Nicholas might have wanted to talk to me about. I'd shut him down, which felt like the right thing to do at the time. Now, I couldn't stop wishing I'd listened to what he'd had to say.

"Do you enjoy it too?" Ethan met my eyes.

My mind raced as I tried to figure out what he'd been talking about. "Uh, sure." I forced a smile.

"Really? I didn't think you would. I've never seen you party much."

"Oh, right...well, now and then." I shrugged.

"So now and then you like to get completely blasted and walk around campus naked?" He raised an eyebrow.

"What?" My eyes widened.

"Exactly." He frowned. "I knew that you weren't listening to anything I said."

"I'm sorry."

He looked out through the window of the bus, then glanced back at me. "I get it."

"You do?"

"Sure." He rested his hand on mine. "I'm no Nicholas Holden."

"Ethan, it's not that."

"It is." He met my eyes. "I can't expect to compete with him. So, I'm not going to try. I invited you with me tonight on a date —with me. You said yes. So, if that was a mistake then you can tell me right now and we can just enjoy the evening as nothing more than friends."

"Ethan."

"Wait." He held up a finger. "But if there's some part of you that's curious about me—and maybe even a little interested— then all I ask is that you spend this night with me. Just me. Give me the same chance that you give him."

I bit into my bottom lip. He could have been angry or offended, but if he was, he chose not to show it. Instead, he gave me the chance to make up for my rudeness. I still didn't feel the slightest spark between us, but that didn't mean it couldn't grow.

"I can do that." I looked into his eyes. "I'm sorry for being distracted. I do want to be here with you."

The bus pulled into the parking lot of a wide-open field and the other students began to get off.

"Are you sure?" He tightened his grasp on my hand. "Because I'm really looking forward to spending some time with you."

"Yes. I'm sure."

In that moment, I was sure. I wanted to see where things with Ethan might end up.

TWENTY-NINE

It had been some time since I'd seen a truly wide-open sky. We had driven far enough from the city to actually see a wide expanse of stars. Looking up into that endless expanse reminded me of the time that Nicholas and I had spent together on the platform of the Brooklyn Bridge.

"It's beautiful, isn't it?" Ethan wrapped his hand around mine as we joined the crowd of students gathered in the middle of the field. A few of the teachers began to set up telescopes.

"Yes." I closed my eyes and wished to feel a rush from his touch. Instead, I felt a bit of sweat and a faint tremble. Was he nervous? I opened my eyes again and caught him staring at me.

"It can be a little overwhelming too." He smiled. "We're allowed to wander off to find our own places to stargaze. Would you like to take a walk with me?"

"Yes, I'd like that." I tightened my hand around his and refused to think about Nicholas. Ethan had asked me to spend the evening with him and that was what I intended to do.

"Ethan, check-in in fifteen minutes!" one of the teachers called out to him as Ethan led me toward the distant trees.

"Will do!" Ethan waved to him, then flashed a smile at me.

"I guess we have a time limit. I'll just have to wow you as quickly as possible."

"Wow me?" I laughed.

"I've got to do something to make an impression, right?"

"You're doing pretty good so far." I smiled.

"Great. But good is not good enough." He steered me toward a thin trail that led through the trees.

"Are you sure you know where you're going?"

"I've been here a few times. I spend a lot of time wandering these trails alone." He coughed. "Not that I'm a loner or anything, I mean, I just don't always have someone to walk with."

"You do tonight." I looked over at him and noticed the softness of his expression. He didn't seem to carry any kind of chip on his shoulder. He appeared relaxed and maybe even a little happy.

Not like Nicholas, who seemed constantly on the verge of frustration.

"No." I sighed. *I'm not supposed to be thinking about him.*

"No?" He looked over at me.

"Sorry, thinking out loud." I blushed.

"So, tell me about yourself. What do you like to do?"

"I spend a lot of time trying to raise awareness about the destruction of the rain forest." I grinned. "That's not exactly thrilling, I know."

"It shows you care." He shrugged. "You don't have to. But you take your time to do something generous. That says a lot about you."

"Thanks. What about you?"

"Mostly I do this." He pulled me past the trees to reveal the sky in a small meadow. "The stars just fascinate me."

I looked up at the stars and smiled. "I can see why. They draw you in."

"It's more than that for me." He lowered his voice. "I guess I'm always looking for something."

"Someone to walk with?" I met his eyes.

"Someone to stargaze with." He shrugged then turned to face me. "Someone who will see more than just the sky. Someone who sees more than just some astronomy geek when she looks at me."

"You're not an astronomy geek."

"I am." He smiled. "I'm not afraid to admit it and I don't want to change it. I just want to find someone who can appreciate me for it."

"I'm sure you will."

My heart sank as I saw the hope blossom in his eyes. I didn't mind that he was an astronomy geek or that he didn't look like Nicholas Holden, but no matter how sweet he was or how much I liked the way he talked, nothing stirred inside of me.

"I hope so." He shifted closer to me. "I know when I tried to kiss you the first time, things didn't go very smoothly. Do you think we could try again?"

I stared into his eyes. My instincts told me not to kiss him. They told me that there was nothing between us. But my thoughts reminded me that Nicholas had resisted kissing me. He had walked away from me. Ethan was right there in front of me—a kind and interesting person who wanted a second chance. If only I could feel the same way about him. Maybe a kiss would ignite something between us.

"Yes." I whispered the word as his lips began to drift toward mine.

I braced myself. I felt the urge to back away, even to run, but I ignored it. It was just a kiss and I wanted it to lead to something more.

My lips were just about to touch his when a sharp crack from behind me made me jump and pull away.

"What was that?" Ethan narrowed his eyes as he looked past me into the trees.

"Ethan!" The teacher's voice echoed from the opposite direction. "Let's go!"

"Time is up." Ethan frowned.

"It's okay, we can wait another minute." I wrapped my arms around his neck and pulled him close.

"Ethan!" Another shout.

"Not like this." Ethan smiled as his lips grazed my cheek. "I want our first kiss to be special, not rushed."

I held back a groan. I, the romantic, didn't care about special for once. I just wanted him to kiss me so I could forget all about Nicholas.

Instead, he turned and started back toward the trail.

"We should get back."

"I'll be right there." I sighed.

"I'll wait for you." He turned back to face me.

"No, go ahead. I need a minute or two, okay?" I smiled.

"Oh." His eyes widened. "Oh right, okay. Uh, just watch out for the poison ivy, okay? You know what it looks like, don't you?" He reached into his pockets. "I'm sorry I don't have any tissues with me."

My cheeks burned as I realized what he thought I needed to do.

"I'll be fine, I have some." I stumbled over my words.

"I'll buy you a few minutes." He waved to me, then hurried off to the entrance of the trail.

I closed my eyes as embarrassment washed over me. No, I didn't need to wander off into the woods and relieve myself. I needed to get my head on straight. I couldn't help feeling guilty, as I knew that the reason I wanted to kiss Ethan had nothing to do with him. If only I could convince myself to feel the same way about Ethan that I did about Nicholas, maybe I could move on from it all.

I started to walk toward the trail when I heard another snap not far behind me.

I spun around just in time to catch a flash of movement in the trees.

"Who's there?" My heart raced.

"It's okay." Nicholas stepped out of the trees and held up his hands. "It's just me. I didn't mean to scare you."

"You didn't mean to scare me?" I glared at him. "So you stalked me?" As angry as I was at him, I couldn't ignore the fact that I was thrilled to see him and also a little concerned that he had watched me try to kiss Ethan.

"I wasn't stalking you." He slipped his hands into his pockets. "Not exactly."

"Not exactly? What part of following me around in the woods is not stalking?"

"The part where I'm doing it for your own safety." He frowned. "I need to protect you."

"From who? Ethan? He's the nicest guy I've ever met."

"He does seem nice." Nicholas looked toward the trail, then back at me. "And no, he's not who I'm trying to protect you from." He met my eyes. "I see that you seem to like him."

"Is that why you're here? You found out about my date with Ethan tonight?" I shook my head. "It's not fair, Nicholas. You tell me that nothing can happen between us, and then you have a problem with me showing interest in someone else?"

THIRTY

"I'm here because you're not safe." Nicholas placed his hands on my shoulders and looked into my eyes. "Knowing who I am puts you at risk."

"Enough." I pulled away from him and shook my head. "I don't want to hear anything more about danger, okay? You told me to stay away from you and that's what I'm trying to do, but here you are."

"You have to hear about it." He stepped in front of me as I started to walk away. "Just stop for a second and listen to me."

"No." I stared into his eyes. "I'm not going to listen anymore. Not to a single word. Not unless you plan to tell me the truth. All of it."

"Fine." He closed his eyes.

"What?"

"Fine." He opened his eyes and met mine. "I'm going to tell you everything."

"Candy!" Ethan called from past the tree line. "We have to go!"

My heart skipped a beat as I stared at Nicholas. In that moment I had a choice. I could turn and run for Ethan, leaving behind Nicholas and all of his drama. I could fully invest myself in the possibility of a real relationship with Ethan. He was full of romance and if I just gave him some time, I was sure that I would develop feelings for him.

Or I could give Nicholas one more chance to tell me the truth about everything.

"I'm listening."

He curled his hands around mine and pulled me gently toward him. "You have to understand. I had to keep everything a secret so that I wouldn't put you in danger. But now you are in danger and you can't comprehend how serious it is unless you know everything."

"Tell me."

"I got involved with some things I shouldn't have. I was stupid. I thought it made me a man to go against my father. I didn't think it would be a big deal if I just started hanging around people that I knew he wouldn't want me to be anywhere near. But things got messy real fast. All I did was get in a car with the wrong person. I swear, I had no idea what they were planning to do. I thought this guy was a decent person—that he just had a bad shake in life. Then he stopped at a shop and went in to grab a drink. Next thing I knew, he came out running with a fistful of cash. He jumped into the car and took off."

"He robbed the place?" My eyes widened. "Are you serious?"

"Yes." He frowned. "And that's when I knew that I had to tell my dad the truth about him. But I was already involved. I was in the car with him when he did it. I didn't have any idea what he planned to do, but I was still there. When I told my dad what happened, everything changed. He said that because I was his son, I'd be a huge target for this guy and his entire gang. So, he put me here at Oak Brook under a different name. It's not what I wanted." He frowned. "I didn't want to change schools. I didn't want to lose all my friends. I couldn't even go back to my own home. But it's what he said he had to do in order to protect me. He warned me that if anyone found out who I was, not only would I be in danger, but the person who found out would be too."

"Wow, Nicholas." I stared at him as I processed his words. "You must have been terrified when that happened."

His jaw tensed as he looked down at the ground. "It's not cool to admit it, I know, but I was. But the fear I felt then—well, it was nothing compared to the fear I felt when I found out you came out here tonight."

He brushed his hair back from his eyes. "I'm not going to lie. I didn't like seeing you with Ethan. But that's not why I came here. I was worried that someone would find out what you knew and come after you—to get to me. I just wanted to make sure that you were safe."

He frowned as he looked into my eyes. "Maybe you've moved on and that's probably for the best, but that doesn't change the fact that you're still at risk. That's why I got so upset when I saw you looking at those articles. It wasn't because you wanted to know the truth. I can understand why you wanted to know that. It's because I knew that the moment you found out who I was, you'd be in danger and it would be my fault."

He touched my cheek as he searched my eyes. "I never wanted to put you in danger. All of the other girls I've been with —we never got close enough for them to have any idea who I was. But you..." He sighed as he let his hand fall back to his side. "Like I said, you're different. I'm sorry. I never should have let this happen to you."

"Nico." I whispered his name as I took his hand. "It's not your fault."

"It is." His voice softened as well. "All of it's my fault. I never should have started things with you, but I just couldn't look away. Now I'm going to have to tell my dad what you know. I'll probably have to leave the school. I just couldn't let you think that I just disappeared."

"Candy!" Ethan's voice was closer this time.

Nicholas looked in the direction of his voice, then looked back at me. "You should get back to him." He tipped his head to the side as he stared at me. "I just want you to be happy, Candy. I'm sorry that I came into your life and complicated things." He drew a shaky breath, then frowned. "Actually, that's another lie. I never wanted to put you in danger, but I'll never be sorry for the time that we had together." He gave my hand a subtle squeeze. "Stay with the group, okay? Don't go out anywhere alone."

"Nicholas, wait." I tried to hold onto his hand as he pulled it away and stepped back into the trees.

"You'd better get back." He nodded toward the trail. "I'll watch to make sure you make it back safe."

"Nicholas." I started to walk toward him.

"Candy!" Ethan appeared at the end of the trail and waved to me. "Let's go! The bus is leaving!"

My heart sank as I stared into Nicholas's eyes. Hidden by the trees, Ethan couldn't see him, but I could. It made my stomach twist into knots to think of Nicholas watching me walk away with Ethan.

"I'm not sorry either, Nico." I spoke just loud enough for Nicholas to hear, then I turned and hurried over to Ethan.

"What's going on? Are you alright?" Ethan frowned as he draped his arm around my shoulders.

My muscles tensed as I became aware that Nicholas had to watch Ethan embrace me. Should I pull away?

What was the point? Nicholas would be leaving the school for his own safety. He would disappear somewhere under a new name and I would be nothing but a memory to him. Hopefully, a good one.

I understood now why Nicholas couldn't tell me the truth. It wasn't about his trying to hide things from me, it was about his trying to keep me safe. My heart softened at the thought. But how I felt about him didn't change anything. He was still out of my reach.

"Yes, I'm fine." I glanced back briefly over my shoulder, then I met Ethan's eyes. "I'm sorry. I just got a little lost."

THIRTY-ONE

On the drive back to the school I leaned my head against the window and started to doze off. The past few days had exhausted me. As my mind drifted between being awake and sleep, my thoughts filled with memories of Nicholas.

Now that I understood why he was so determined to protect me, I understood why he'd had to lie to me. He lived a life I couldn't even imagine. He'd gotten himself caught up in a bad situation and had been paying the price ever since.

"Is she asleep?" A soft voice spoke from the seat in front of us.

I kept my eyes closed.

"I think so," Ethan whispered.

"You were gone the whole time. You missed everything. I thought you were excited about tonight."

"I was." He cleared his throat. "There will be other nights."

"Was it worth it? Did you get your kiss?"

"Sh!" Ethan shifted in his seat.

"What? It's what you wanted, right? You gave up your whole night; I hope you at least got that."

"We had a moment." Ethan sighed. "Not that it's any of your business."

"Of course it's my business. I'll be the one mopping up your tears when she bails on you for another bad boy."

"Sh!" Ethan's tone grew sharper. "Just drop it before you wake her up."

I did my best not to react to the conversation. I didn't know who Ethan was speaking to, but I did know that she was right. At least for the moment. I wished it wasn't the case, but while I sat beside him, all I could think about was Nicholas.

"Sure, I'll be quiet."

"Savannah, don't be like that."

She didn't say another word.

I wondered who this Savannah was and why Ethan was so concerned with what she had to say. I searched my memory for any recognition of her voice, but I couldn't place her.

After a few minutes of silence, I opened my eyes and caught sight of the top of a head. Her black hair was a bit mussed. She didn't turn her head.

I glanced over at Ethan, who was staring down at his phone. My stomach churned. How fair was this to him? Yes, he deserved to have someone who actually wanted to be with him, not someone who was just hoping that a spark would distract her from someone else.

"Candy?" He looked over at me.

I quickly closed my eyes. For the remainder of the drive I continued to pretend to sleep, but my thoughts swirled instead. I kept running over in my mind how the night had played out. Ethan had invited me along on an important night for him, and I'd only been focused on Nicholas.

The bus pulled to a stop and I realized that I would have to finally face the truth. I had a decision to make, and the longer I put it off, the less chance there was that I could make it, because the longer I allowed myself to toy with the heart of an innocent person, the less chance there was that I could ever call myself a decent person again.

I watched as the girl in front of us stepped into the aisle of the bus. Her plain face was bare of any make-up. Her hair looked like it had barely been brushed. Her clothes hung from her body, offering no hint to her figure. She glanced so briefly at me that I didn't have a chance to meet her eyes.

I noticed that she didn't say a word to Ethan as she left the bus and we stepped off behind her. As I continued to watch her, I realized that I had no idea who she was. Obviously, she went to the same school as me. How could I never have noticed her or met her?

"Hey." Ethan drew me away from the group of students. "Can we take a quick walk?"

"Sure." I did my best to ignore the feeling of dread that swelled up within me. Would I be able to do the right thing?

"Did you have a nice nap?" He grinned as he guided me toward the row of statues that lined the courtyard.

"I'm sorry I passed out on you."

My heart pounded as I caught sight of the statue that Nicholas had damaged. I suddenly understood his desire to change it. He felt pressured to be perfect due to the job his father held, but he'd made mistakes, just like everyone did in life, and those mistakes left him feeling flawed.

I understood how that felt. As I met Ethan's eyes, I'd never felt more flawed. There was a time, not long before, that I considered myself to be a kind and thoughtful person. But now, I saw myself very differently.

"I don't mind. I think you needed the rest." He took my hand. "Thanks for coming with me tonight."

"I'm sorry I wasn't better company." I focused on his hand

around mine. I hoped for even the slightest spark. Instead, all I felt was the faint shiver in his hand and a hint of sweat.

"I enjoyed myself." He looked into my eyes. "I just wanted some time with you." He stepped closer to me. "I know we got interrupted this evening. But now we're all alone—just us."

Those words sent a shower of sparks through me. I recalled Nicholas murmuring them to me when we were alone. I remembered the thrill I felt at the thought of us disappearing from the rest of the world. But when Ethan said them, they were just words.

"Ethan, we need to talk." My cheeks flushed.

"What is it? Just be honest with me."

"Ethan, I think you're a great guy. You're kind and sweet."

"Oh, the great guy speech." He shoved his hands in his pockets and sighed as he looked up at the sky. "Like I haven't heard that a thousand times."

"Ethan, it's not like that."

"It's exactly like that." He stared straight into my eyes. "Please, don't stress yourself over a longwinded speech. I've heard every version of this. Ethan, you're a great guy, but we just don't have a connection. Ethan, I really enjoy spending time with you, but just as friends. Or the worst...Ethan, I wish I could feel that way about you, but I just don't." He pursed his lips as he looked at me. "Trust me, I don't want to be with someone who has to talk themselves into spending time with me."

"I'm sorry." I looked down at my feet as guilt rippled through me. "I wish I could explain it."

"You don't need to explain." He took a step back. "I can't hold a candle to Nicholas. And you know what? It's ridiculous that I even tried. I hope that he doesn't hurt you. You seem like a really good person, Candy. Just be careful."

"How can you do that?"

"Do what?"

"Be so kind to me even after I ruined your evening? I had no idea how important it was to you."

"So you weren't asleep." He smiled.

"No. I was just being a coward."

"You could have let this go on for a long time. I would have kept hanging on you—hoping. I appreciate that you made it clear to me how you feel." He shrugged. "I'm not going to say it doesn't hurt. But I'm used to it."

I watched as a ripple of pain flickered across his face. My heart softened as I recognized that pain.

"You know, Ethan, I've been waiting for a long time too. I kept hoping I would find someone—anyone—who I could have that head-over-heels connection with. I didn't think it would ever happen."

"And you really think you have that with Nicholas?"

"I think I have something that I've never felt before. Something that I've hoped for. My point is that when I least expected it, it happened. It's going to happen for you too."

"Sure." He nodded, then looked toward the dorms. "I should go. Good luck with Nicholas, Candy." He turned and walked off toward the dorms.

I felt a faint urge to call him back. How stupid could I be? This wonderful person wanted to be part of my life, while Nicholas didn't. Sure, he had good reason to want to avoid me, but that didn't change the fact that he didn't want to be with me.

As I started toward the dorms as well, I heard a voice from behind one of the statues.

"Head over heels, huh?"

THIRTY-TWO

My heart skipped a beat at the sound of his voice. My knees weakened. I fought through the dizziness that swept over me to focus a glare on him as he stepped out from behind the statue.

"Following me again?"

"I just wanted to make sure that you got home safe." He met my eyes.

"That excuse doesn't make you any less of a stalker." I crossed my arms. "Besides, anything you heard was just my way of letting Ethan down easily."

"Oh?" He tipped his head back as he looked at me. "So, you were lying to him?"

"It doesn't matter, does it?"

"It matters to me." He glanced away briefly toward the crowd of students still dispersing to the dorms, then looked back at me. "A lot."

"It shouldn't. Like you said, it's impossible for us to be together. In fact, I've made things even worse for you, haven't I?" I frowned. "If I hadn't been so nosey, you wouldn't have to leave the school. I exposed you. I put you in a lot of danger. You shouldn't care what I think about you."

"I do." He caught my hand and looked into my eyes. "I care."

I stared back at him as my heart raced. It was strange how I would do just about anything to avoid a kiss from Ethan, but when Nicholas held my hand, I wanted to kiss him more than anything.

He stepped closer to me.

I breathed in his scent. I sensed the nearness of his skin. I bit into my bottom lip.

His fingertips settled against my cheek.

I felt the heat from his touch spread far from their reach. I closed my eyes.

"Candy." His breath tickled against my lips as he whispered. "I do care."

I shivered, then drew a breath that interlaced with his own. How close was he? Just a tilt of my chin and my lips would most likely touch his. Frustration bolted through me and I took a step back.

His hand slipped from my cheek to curve around the back of my neck just as I felt a graze of his lips.

The light touch sent euphoria through my senses and almost an instant frustration. I took another step back and pulled away from his touch.

"Don't."

"Why not?" He frowned as his eyes swept over me. "I saw you try to kiss Ethan. I know you don't feel about him the way you feel about me. So why not?"

"I can't." My chest ached. I hated myself for my own words. "Nico, I just can't. Don't you see that? You're going to disappear." I fought to ignore the rush of tears that threatened. "You're right. I can't change how I feel about you. I tried. I tried to feel the right things for the right person, but I can't. That's the problem."

"That I'm not the right person? Because I've made some stupid mistakes." He shook his head. "I know that."

"Because you are the right person." I stared into his eyes. "Because you are exactly the person that I've been waiting for all this time. You make my heart race just by hearing you speak. You occupy my mind from the time I wake up in the morning until the time I'm able to fall asleep at night. When you look at me, there isn't a single thing that would make me want to look away."

"And?"

"And that's the problem." I took another step back. "It's my desire for you that caused this whole mess. Isn't it? I fell for you, and because of that I wouldn't take no for an answer. You tried to warn me, but I pushed and pushed. You tried to protect me and yourself, but I was too stupid to see that. So, I pushed even harder until I managed to get us both into a bad situation. Your dad—he is doing everything he can to protect you, but because of me, he's going to have to come up with a new plan."

"You're not the one that started this, Candy. Don't you remember?" A smile tugged at the corner of his lips. "I saw you first."

"You saw another girl, just like the rest of them. You saw someone that you wanted to have a little fun with." I shrugged as a wave of sadness caused my voice to shudder. "I saw someone that I couldn't live without. I didn't mean to. I didn't expect it. But there you were, and once I saw you, I couldn't un-see you. I wish I had. I wish I'd just walked away. I wish that I'd been strong enough to resist the way that I felt about you, so that neither of us would be stuck in this situation."

"No one has ever seen me that way." He held his hand out to me. "I've never seen anyone the way that I see you. You may be right, I may need to move on, I may not get to see you again for a while. But we still have right now. We can still be just us, together, in this moment. Isn't that worth something to you?"

I couldn't resist taking his hand. My thumb stroked across the back of it. I fought the urge to pull him close and kiss him the way I had been longing to for what seemed like an eternity.

"It's worth everything, Nico. But it's not going to be enough. I'm going to want more. I'm going to want to hold onto you and never let you go. I don't think I can be strong enough to let you go. So, I'm trying to control myself now, before things go too far, before there's no turning back for me. Your safety is more important to me than anything I might feel when we kiss. It's more important to me to know that you're not in danger than to know where you are or to be able to reach you."

I drew a sharp breath. "Trust me, I'm pretty sure this is the hardest thing that I've ever had to do. I'm not built to be brave. I'm built to defend the rain forest and the environment, not to fight against every instinct in my body that tells me kissing you would be the most magical experience of my life—an experience I probably wouldn't ever get to have again."

"You're thinking too much." He slid his arms around my waist and pulled my body close to his. "Just tell me I can. Just tell me." He edged his lips toward mine.

I felt my world spin as his body suddenly surrounded mine. I could already taste the softness of his lips. It was sweeter than anything I'd ever craved. But even as my nerves exploded with urgency, I clenched my jaw and tipped my head to the side.

"Please don't, Nico."

"Fine." He released me and created space between us. "Fine. But this is your decision, not mine. You think you're doing what's best for both of us. But you're not. You're just too scared to find out where a kiss would lead."

"Aren't you?" I met his eyes. "Isn't that why you're going to leave the school and go into hiding again? Because you're too scared? It's not like I have control over that."

"Neither do I!" He narrowed his eyes. "I didn't ask for any of this! I didn't want to be imprisoned by one stupid mistake!"

"And I don't want to be the mistake that gets you killed!" My throat ached with the panic that coursed through me. "Can't you see that, Nico? I don't want to be the reason that you make a choice that you can never take back!"

"The only mistake I'm afraid of making is missing out on the chance to be with you." Nico stared hard into my eyes. "But I can see that you don't feel the same way. So, you're probably right. It's for the best that we don't see each other again. You may think you're head over heels, but you're lying to yourself. Because if you felt the way I do, nothing would stop you."

THIRTY-THREE

I knew that I should say something. There were hundreds of words swirling through my mind. But none of them made sense.

As Nicholas spread his arms wide and backed away from me, I wanted to wrap my arms around him and pull him back. But my body remained as frozen as my tongue.

"Now is the time." He held my gaze. "If you're going to ask me to stay, this is when you should do it. I will stay. All you have to do is ask."

My lips tingled with the desire to ask—maybe even beg—him to stay. But instead, I watched him slip further and further away. How could I do anything else? Asking him to stay would put him in danger.

He claimed that he would stay, but I knew that would only lead to disaster. Was he right? Had I fooled myself into thinking that I had stronger feelings for him than I actually did?

With my heart in my throat, I watched him disappear. I heard the sound of his footsteps as he walked further and further away.

Tears sprang up, but I didn't allow them to fall. How could

I? What right did I have to cry, when I'd been the one to let him walk away?

Confused and frustrated, I walked back to the dorm. I'd started out the night with the hope that I'd start a new, accessible, and reasonable relationship with Ethan. Instead, I was even more lost than ever and definitely alone.

I stared at the ceiling all night. I memorized the cracks and faded paint. As tired as I was, all I wanted to do was sleep and just have a brief break from my mind. But I couldn't because every time I closed my eyes, I saw him walking away.

By the time my alarm went off, I wished I never had to leave the room again. If I could just hole up there, I'd never have to face the rest of my life without Nicholas being part of it. My stomach ached at the thought of finding a way to let go of him.

As I walked toward my first class of the day, I noticed the couples around me. Two people snuggled up together by the water fountain. Shared laughter over a shared joke from a couple not far from the bathroom. Two people locking eyes across the hallway, their instant smiles a dead giveaway that romance was blossoming. And me, feeling gutted, quite obviously alone.

Right then I made a decision.

I'd been so focused on finding a real romance for the past few months that I'd let myself lose sight of everything else. I had my whole life in front of me—so many good moments, so many experiences that I had no way to prepare for. I didn't want to lose out on them just because I didn't have someone by my side.

Meeting Nicholas had launched me into a whirlwind fantasy, but there wasn't anything real about it. The one thing about romance movies and romance books was that they always came to an end. But the life of those characters still continued on. What happened then? What happened when things didn't go as they were supposed to, when outside circumstances prevented them from being together? Real life was full of bumps and potholes.

The best way to avoid heartbreak was to protect my heart in the first place. I suddenly understood my friends who fought so hard to avoid being in a relationship. They knew something that I hadn't figured out. Falling in love and losing that love hurt more than any words could describe.

As I settled at my desk and barely heard the teacher's words, I knew that I didn't want romance anymore. In fact, I might not ever want it again. I wanted to be safe from the kind of pain that kept me up all night. I wanted to dream of things other than Nicholas's smile and his touch. I wanted to be free of the mixture of guilt and regret that I felt.

By the time I made it to lunch, I felt determined not to involve myself in the slightest hint of romance. Of course, sitting down across from Ethan didn't make that easy.

"Oh. You sit here now?" I met his eyes.

"I hope you don't mind." He shrugged. "I've gotten to know everyone pretty well and since you made it clear that there's nothing between us, I didn't think you'd care."

"It's fine. Of course." I smiled at him. Sure, I wanted to be reminded that I'd tried to use him to distract myself from Nicholas.

Maybe it was a good thing to be reminded of what love had turned me into.

Or maybe it wasn't love at all, like Nicholas claimed. Maybe it was just infatuation. Either way, all of it was over and I was determined to keep it that way.

"You okay?" Jenny leaned close to me.

"Sure, fine. Why?" I met her eyes.

"You just look different to me."

"I haven't been sleeping much." I wiped my hands across my eyes. "I probably have bags under my eyes."

"I don't think that's it." She frowned. "Want to meet up later? Talk about it?"

As I stared at my friend, I wondered whether there was anything to talk about. How could she understand what I was going through when she'd found someone to be with? I didn't want anyone to talk me out of the decision I'd made.

"Actually, I have a protest to go to this afternoon. I'm going to be pretty busy making signs until then."

"Oh, want any help?"

"It's okay." I forced a smile, then stood up and left the table. I wasn't hungry anyway.

As I headed to the library, it shocked me to think that I'd almost forgotten about the protest. I'd played a part in organizing it and due to the chaos that had taken over my life, I'd almost missed it.

I closed myself off in one of the rooms in the library and spread poster board across the table.

As I began to create signs for the protest, I thought about the things that were important to me. Saving the rain forest. Helping other people to focus on protecting the planet we shared. There were lots of things in life that didn't require a partner, and I was ready to dive as deep as I could into them.

I became so engrossed in creating the posters that I didn't notice when the door to the room swung open. I didn't even sense the presence of another person until he cleared his throat.

I looked up to see Nicholas right in front of me.

"No."

"No?" He stared at me.

"I mean, what are you doing here?" My heart raced, as if everything I'd decided had never even been thought about.

"I wanted to say goodbye." He brushed his hair back from his eyes. "I know last night things were tense. I just couldn't leave here without seeing you again."

"Now you've seen me." I clenched my jaw.

"I said some things that weren't fair." He tried to meet my eyes. "I want to apologize for that."

"Don't bother." I stared down at the posters in front of me. "You weren't wrong. I was fooling myself. There was never anything real between us."

"How can you say that?" His voice tightened as he leaned his hands against the table and looked straight at me.

"That's what you said last night, isn't it?" I forced myself to look into his eyes. "That I couldn't possibly be in love with you? I'm just agreeing with you."

"I just don't want things to end this way between us."

"There's nothing to end." I picked up a marker. "If you don't mind, I'm pretty busy."

"Candy."

"Goodbye, Nicholas." I stared down at the poster in front of me.

As he turned toward the door it took all my strength to remain in my chair. When I heard the door creak, I couldn't resist looking up.

"I hope you find somewhere safe, Nico."

He looked back at me and for a second I saw a flicker of heat in his eyes before he pulled the door closed behind him.

THIRTY-FOUR

That look in his eyes—it haunted me all afternoon. As I loaded my posters into a cab, I couldn't get it out of my mind. I hadn't meant to be cruel. But I had to find a way to protect myself.

On the ride to the protest, I tried to convince myself that I'd done the right thing. Nicholas needed some closure. It would be easier for him to walk away if he thought there was nothing holding him back. More than anything I wanted him to be safe. If that meant having to hurt him a little, then that was what had to happen.

But did I mean what I said? As I set up my signs and greeted a few of my friends, I couldn't get my mind off him. What if that really was the last time I saw him? The thought made my mind spin with fear. How could I have let him walk away like that?

I remembered the first night I met him. How he'd run from me and escaped through the hole in the fence. I'd let him get away then, not because I was afraid, but because a part of me already knew that I didn't really want to see him get into trouble.

"Candy!" Apple waved to me as she ran up to the group of

protesters. "I'm sorry I'm late." She held out her phone to me. "But have you seen this?"

"What is it?" I took her phone from her.

The moment I saw the news article my heart dropped. The headline read *Police Commissioner's Son Agrees to Testify* in bold lettering. Beneath it was a picture of Nico and his father.

"This can't be right." I looked up at Apple. "He'll be in so much danger if he does this."

"Did you know about this?"

"Sort of." I frowned.

"I had no idea that he'd been hiding out at the school. As soon as I saw this, I thought of you. You saw something in Nicholas that none of the rest of us did Candy. Who knew he was such a brave person?"

"He is brave, isn't he?" I stared at the picture again. "Or stupid."

"Is he doing it for you?" She looked into my eyes as I glanced up.

"Of course not."

"You don't have to lie to me." Apple took her phone back from me. "I know that you two had something going on. You can tell me that I'm wrong until you turn blue, but I saw the look in your eyes whenever he was around. When I heard he was leaving, I was surprised. When I saw this, I knew you had to see it."

"Thanks for showing me." I shook my head. "But there's nothing between us. I thought..." I sighed, then closed my eyes. "I don't know exactly what I thought. But I was wrong."

"Are you sure about that?" She swept her gaze around the gathering of people, then looked back at me. "It's easy to know what to believe in when it's something like this, something so clear. The rain forest is a beautiful place, but it's also vitally important to our world. Who wouldn't want to protect it? It's a lot harder to fight for something that is less clear. It's a lot harder to hear your heart when there are all kinds of opinions drowning it out."

As she blended in with the other protesters, I tried to imagine what Nicholas must be thinking. Why would he expose himself that way? Why would he put himself at so much risk?

I pulled out my phone and dialed his number. Instead of hearing his voicemail, I heard a message declaring the phone number out of service.

I closed my eyes as I remembered the way I'd treated him in the library. Of course he didn't want to hear from me. I'd made it absolutely clear that I wanted nothing to do with him.

Sick to my stomach, I tried to focus on the protest. But Apple's words sank in. Yes, it was easy to fight for something that was so clearly right. But what about fighting for something that might end in my getting hurt? What about fighting for something that I wanted so badly that it terrified me?

As I collected the signs after the protest, I realized it was most likely already too late. Anything I might have wanted to happen between Nicholas and me would now never happen.

As Apple climbed into the cab beside me, I saw the faint smile on her lips.

"Did you enjoy the protest?"

"Huh?" She looked at me, then smiled wider. "Sorry, I just got an invite to go out for dinner tonight."

"Of course you did." I forced a smile in return. Couples. They were everywhere.

I leaned my head back against the seat and watched as the city slipped past me. It wasn't until I'd explored it with Nicholas that I even really noticed it. I hadn't experienced the beauty of it until I'd looked at it through his eyes.

I recalled the moment I'd seen the statue he'd destroyed. I wanted to be outraged, but instead I'd seen his message. Perfection has no place in life. The bumps and the potholes are part of the journey, but if all we ever see are the angelic smiles and the smooth wide-open paths, then that's what we think it should be.

"There's nothing smooth about it."

"Huh?" Apple looked up from her phone.

"Nothing." I bit into my bottom lip. I'd wanted to smooth the rough edges. I'd wanted to protect Nicholas by removing all potential of harm from around him, by removing myself. I'd wanted to protect myself as well—from the moment that he would inevitably say goodbye to me. But all that protection had only prevented me from seeing what I really wanted.

Just like for the rain forest, I wanted to fight. I wanted to protest against the unfairness of the world around us and pull him into the comfort of my arms, to help soothe the wounds he'd collected from the bumps and potholes along the way.

And maybe he could soothe a few of mine.

But that chance had passed. Hadn't it?

"Stop!"

The driver looked in the rearview mirror. "What?"

"Stop the car!" I smacked the back of the seat in front of me. "Stop it right now, I need to get out!"

"Here?" He frowned. "We're in the middle of the Brooklyn Bridge."

"Please!" I stared into his eyes.

"Candy have you lost your mind?" Apple frowned. "We have to get back to Oak Brook."

"No, not yet." I shifted the signs closer to her. "Can you make sure these get put away for me, please?"

"Yes, I can, but where are you going? I can come with you."

As the cab pulled to a stop, I popped the door open and hopped out. "I have to do this alone, Apple. Enjoy your dinner!" I waved to her as I ran along the walking path of the bridge.

Was it possible that he would be there? I ran straight for the middle of the bridge and looked up.

My heart sank as I saw that the platform was gone. The repair had been completed.

Nicholas wasn't sitting up there waiting for me. In fact, he most likely wasn't anywhere waiting for me. He'd made a decision to move on with his life because I'd given him no other choice.

I sank to my knees as my chest ached with pain. I'd played it safe as usual and it had cost me everything. As tears slipped down my cheeks I remembered the comfort of his arms around me.

How could I have given that up so easily? Why hadn't I bothered to fight for it?

THIRTY-FIVE

After a cab ride back to Oak Brook, I couldn't bring myself to go back to the dorm. I'd already missed dinner and I knew that Apple would have a lot of questions. I wasn't ready to answer them.

I'd started out the morning determined not to think about romance or to long for it. But now, all I could think about was Nicholas. Would he be safe if he testified? With his name and face out there, would he ever be safe even after the trial?

I walked through the courtyard in the direction of the statues. The moment that I saw them, I knew that I had to see Nicholas's statue again. As I walked toward it, I heard a loud scraping sound.

"What's going on here?" I watched as one of the maintenance workers struggled to position a statue.

"Just replacing one of the statues." He looked over at me. "I'm guessing you have no idea who damaged it?"

"No." I stared at the statue. "It's exactly like the old one."

"Sure looks like it." He nodded.

"I don't get it. How did the artist create a new one so fast?" I narrowed my eyes. "And so perfect?"

"Oh, no artist. It's factory made." He slapped the arm of the statue. "But it sure is heavy."

"It's made in a factory?" My eyes widened.

"Sure. We just ordered a new one." He shrugged, then turned and walked away.

I stared at the statue. It looked so strange to me now. Why put statues like that in the middle of a school courtyard? Why did we as young students need to walk past perfection each day and think that was what we needed to reach?

I could only imagine how Nicholas felt when he made the mistake he did. With one bad decision, he had put his life at risk and his father's career at risk, and his future had permanently changed. It was a choice made by someone not quite mature enough to understand the far-reaching consequences of his actions.

He'd gotten into the wrong car with the wrong people and he'd been paying for it ever since. His chance at perfection was erased in that moment. But the truth was, it had been erased long before that. In fact, his chance at perfection had never existed in the first place. It didn't exist for anyone.

I pulled out my phone and looked at the picture I'd snapped of the statue he'd damaged. It meant enough to him to try to break the routine, to try to break the pattern of demand for perfection, that he'd risked getting into even more trouble to change it. He'd fought for what he believed in.

Now, I intended to do the same.

I lingered by the storage shed marked "maintenance" and waited for the workers to lock it up for the day.

As I watched them disappear through the gate, my heart began to pound. I'd never done anything wrong before—nothing really wrong anyway. I'd never broken the rules or broken a lock but today, I intended to do both.

I grabbed onto the padlock and tugged at it. I expected it to be impossible to open, but instead it fell open against my palm. My eyes widened as I realized that the workers had forgotten to lock it.

Was this the universe's way of making my task easier? Or was it just luck?

I pulled open the door and stepped inside. Using the flashlight on my phone I searched for what I needed.

When I emerged from the shed again, I felt a rush carry through me. I might get expelled. I might end up with no future. But none of that frightened me enough to stop me. The only thing that frightened me was the thought that I might never get this chance again.

I hurried back toward the courtyard.

With my heart pounding, I stepped up to the new statue. It wasn't really art. It came from a mold in a factory. It wasn't exactly sacred. Yet, I still felt hesitant as I looked at it. I'd never destroyed anything before. I'd never scrawled on a wall with spray paint or stomped on someone's sandcastle.

I turned the drill on. As I felt its power vibrate against my palm, my stomach flipped. What was I thinking? How could I even hope to recreate what Nicholas had done? He was an artist. I was a novice at best.

My hand trembled as I pointed the drill at the statue. As the bit touched the stone, I heard footsteps behind me.

I took a sharp breath and lowered the drill. "Who's there?" I glanced around for any sign of another person. Was I about to be caught before I could even begin to fight?

"What are you doing?" Nicholas stepped out of the shadows.

"Nico." I stared into his eyes. "Is it safe for you to be out here?"

"Is it safe for you to be doing that?" He winced as he placed his hand over mine and steered the drill away from my side. "You're going to hurt yourself."

"I was just trying to create it again." I frowned. "I mean, I know I couldn't make it exactly like you did, but I just wanted to show you that I can see it now."

"See what?" He turned the drill off and set it on the ground.

"How perfection is a problem."

"Is that all you can see?" He caressed my cheek and continued to hold my gaze.

"I can see that you fought for me. Even though you probably shouldn't have. But I don't understand why you agreed to testify. Don't you know how much danger you're in now?"

"None." He let his hand rest on my shoulder. "I agreed to testify and the guy who was after me agreed to make a deal. So now, he's not after me anymore. He has bigger fish to fry."

"Does that mean you don't have to leave?" My heart skipped a beat.

"I don't have to." He frowned. "But it still might be for the best."

"Why?" I searched his eyes. "If you don't have to leave, why would you want to?"

"I don't want to." He hooked his fingers around mine and shook his head. "It's the last thing that I want."

"Then why?"

"Maybe because you were about to slaughter an innocent statue." He tipped his head toward the drill.

"It's not innocent." I glanced at it. "It's a lie."

"Maybe." He stepped closer to me. "I never wanted to hurt you, Candy."

"I know that."

"Do you?" He brushed my hair back from my shoulder and cupped the back of my neck with the warmth of his palm.

"Because you seemed pretty certain you didn't want me around."

"I thought I was protecting you." I sighed. "I thought that the best way to keep you safe was to keep you as far away from me as possible. I still don't understand why you decided to testify."

"I realized that losing out on a chance to be with you is far more dangerous than anyone hunting me down. But I didn't want to put you at risk. So I did what I had to do to try to make sure you would be safe. I can't guarantee it won't blow back in my face later, but for now, there's no bounty on my head."

"I'm sorry." I looked down at my feet.

"What could you have to be sorry for?" He gently guided my chin upward so that he could look into my eyes.

"I didn't fight for you the way you fought for me."

"You fought for me harder than anyone else ever has." He searched my eyes. "You fought to see the real me, when no one else has bothered to look past the surface. Whether we can be together or not, I will always be grateful for that."

My heart pounded with desire as his fingertips lingered on the curve of my chin. I could detect the heat from his thumb as it swept just beneath my bottom lip. I ached to finally kiss him.

"Nico." I gazed at him. "Please stay."

THIRTY-SIX

"I don't want you to think that you have to do something like this—to be with me." He gestured to the statue. "I don't want to change you, Candy. I want you to be exactly who you are."

"I want you to do the same." I touched his cheek. "Nico, will you stay?"

"You haven't asked me." His eyes settled on mine.

"I just did." I frowned.

"Not really. You didn't." His lips twitched a little.

"Nico, please stay." I searched his eyes. "I'm asking you."

"No, you're not." His lips spread into a light smile.

"If you don't want to stay, then just say so." I frowned as I let my hands fall back to my sides. "I don't want to play games."

"Neither do I." He locked his eyes to mine as he caught my hands and held them tight. "So, ask me. For real this time."

Frustrated, I started to jerk my hands free from his grasp. How could he possibly not just answer me? He acted as if he wanted to stay but claimed I hadn't asked.

And here I was again, ready to walk away. Ready to break free and run from the hard parts.

As I stared back into his eyes and his hands relaxed around

mine, suddenly I understood exactly how to ask. My heart slowed down to a steady hard pounding. The air around me became rich with scents I hadn't noticed before. The sounds of the night echoed through my ears. Everything seemed to slow down. I watched as a few strands of his hair tickled at the curve of his eyebrow and his lips continued to dance between a serious expression and a faint smile.

He was just so beautiful. He didn't want to hear any more words from me. He didn't want to wait a second longer to know how I really felt. He wanted me to ask him to stay in a way that showed him exactly what I wanted.

"Nico." I shifted closer to him as his name rolled off of the tip of my tongue and floated in the electrified air between us. "Please stay." As the last word slipped out, I touched my lips to his.

I felt him take a sharp breath, as if he was surprised, then a moment later his arms swept around me and he kissed me in return.

As I tumbled headfirst into the most passionate kiss I'd ever experienced, my entire body came alive with the desire for it to never stop. The hairs on my arm rose up, I rocked forward onto the tips of my toes, and I felt the subtle pressure of his fingertips against the small of my back.

A light engulfed me from the inside out, and in that moment, as my mind spun with a mixture of colors and sensations, I understood what it meant to be head over heels in love. It wasn't about certain words, or the right timing. It was about the blending of two people so completely invested in one another's well-being that they would do anything for each other.

I swept my hands back through his hair and curved my arms around his neck. I wanted to hold onto him for as long as I could.

When he finally broke the kiss, I heard him pull in an uneven breath, then his lips found mine again and I swam right back in. As the force of my desire swept over me, my knees weakened and I stumbled back a few steps. I felt my back collide with the new statue that had replaced the damaged one. Somewhere in the back of my mind it registered that it tilted a bit, but that didn't break through the mass of wild thoughts that had been set free by the kiss we shared.

"Candy." He broke free again and this time drew in a few breaths as he looked into my eyes. "I will stay. I promise."

"I will fight for you, I promise." I stroked his cheek and savored the warmth of his skin under my fingertips. "Nico, I would do anything to keep you safe. I hope you know that."

"I hope you know the same." He tightened his arms around my waist. "I promise, no more climbing to the top of the Brooklyn Bridge. No more taking chances that could get either of us into trouble."

"I don't mind getting into a little bit of trouble. As long as it's with you." I grinned.

"Are you sure about that?" He raised an eyebrow. "Because I know a great spot on the Statue of Liberty."

"What?" I laughed.

"Don't worry." He pinned me close to him and pressed his lips against my cheek. Then he whispered in my ear. "I won't let you fall."

"I'm pretty sure it's too late for that." I nestled my lips against the curve of his neck. "I'm pretty sure I've already fallen —head over heels."

"Then I'll fall with you." He leaned his head back and looked into my eyes. "Every step of the way."

"Oh, Nico." I smiled as another rush of passion washed over me. I wrapped my arms around his neck and pulled him forward for another kiss.

As I tugged him, he stumbled just a step, then caught himself on the statue behind me.

As our lips collided, I felt the world spin around me. I really was falling. It took me a second to realize that it wasn't just in my mind.

"Candy!" Nicholas swept me back against him and took a step back just as the newly placed statue tumbled over behind us.

The perfect stone figure shattered against the cobblestone of the courtyard the moment it struck it.

"Oh no!" I gasped and laughed at the same time.

"I guess we should have been more careful." He winced.

"Nico." I looked into his eyes as I heard footsteps in the distance.

"Yes, Candy?" He leaned in for another kiss.

"No time for that! We have to run!" I grabbed his hand and tugged him forward.

As we ran through the courtyard, I remembered the rush of running through Brooklyn with him. A little bit of trouble wasn't the worst thing in the world. A few rough edges and some potholes left me with the kind of wounds that made me even more aware of just how special it was to have someone who could soothe them.

I pulled him through the hole in the fence.

"Candy, where are we going?" He laughed.

"Anywhere." I smiled as I looked back at him, feeling maybe the happiest I'd ever felt in my entire life. "As long as I'm with you."

EPILOGUE

"No talking!" The teacher smacked her hand against the desk and glared at us.

I tried to hide my smile.

Detention was my favorite place to be with Nicholas. As I shuffled through the papers on my desk, he glanced at me and winked.

We didn't often end up in detention together anymore, but now and then we managed to stumble into trouble. This time it happened because of a protest that got out of hand. I had no idea that inspiring a sit-in in the library would cause so much trouble. But it did and it landed us both in detention yet again, along with a few other people.

As I tucked the brochures into my backpack, I noticed a girl in the corner of the room. She had her desk pulled away from the others. She stared listlessly out through the window into the courtyard. I vaguely remembered seeing her at the sit-in. She hadn't said a word, but she'd sat with us.

The bell rang to release us from detention and Nicholas grabbed my hand. He tugged me out of the room and into the courtyard. As he spun me back against the wall, I tilted my lips up to meet his. The kiss made me forget everything for a few moments, then I broke it. I saw her walking across the courtyard in the direction of the dormitories.

"Savannah!" I pulled free of Nicholas and jogged over to her.

"Yeah?" She turned to look at me but didn't smile.

"Thanks for being there today. I know that you didn't have to be."

"You've been so nice to me." She shrugged. "Besides, it was for a good cause."

"I didn't see you at lunch today. I thought you were sitting with us now."

"I thought maybe I shouldn't." She shrugged. "I do better on my own."

"That's not really true." I met her eyes. "Sometimes it's easier to pretend that it is, but it's never actually true, is it?"

"For me it is." She slipped her hands into her pockets. "I mean, it has been in the past anyway."

"I hope that changes." I frowned. "I know when you've been hurt, things can seem pointless. But they do eventually get better."

"You know, huh?" She looked past me at Nicholas, where he still waited for me. "I hope you won't blame me for thinking that maybe you don't."

"Is this about Ethan?" I smiled. "I saw you two together today."

"We're just friends." She turned away as she spoke. "Please, I don't want to be anybody's pity project."

"That's not what you are." I took her hand before she could get too far. "Savannah, I promise that's not what you are."

"You should get back." She looked past me again. "Enjoy it. Be happy." She pulled her hand free. "I have to go."

"Savannah, I'm going to find you later. I want to talk."

"Sure." She nodded, then strode off.

As I watched her blend in with the crowd of other students, my heart ached for her. Finding Nicholas was the most wonderful thing I'd ever experienced, but it had also been quite painful. I guessed, from the words I'd heard exchanged between Savannah and Ethan, that it was just as painful for her.

"Everything okay?" Nicholas walked up beside me and draped his arm around my shoulders.

"I hope so." I frowned. "Life certainly isn't perfect, is it?"

"No, it's not." He kissed my cheek and pulled me closer. "But sometimes, it can come pretty close." He looked into my eyes for a long moment, then kissed me.

As I lost myself in the kiss, I savored the rush of euphoria that carried through me. Yes, life could feel pretty perfect, even with all its bumps and potholes.

ALSO BY JILLIAN ADAMS

Amazon.com/author/jillianadams

OAK BROOK ACADEMY SERIES

The New Girl (Sophie and Wes)

Falling for Him (Alana and Mick)

No More Hiding (Apple and Ty)

Worth the Wait (Maby and Oliver)

A Fresh Start (Jennifer and Gabriel)

Taking a Chance (Candy and Nicholas)

Risking it All (Savannah and Ethan)

Time for Healing (Lily and Austin)

Made in the USA
Middletown, DE
04 October 2022

11952217R00126